I KNOW YOUR SECRET

DAPHNE BENEDIS-GRAB

I KNOW YOUR SECRET

BY DAPHNE BENEDIS-GRAB

Scholastic Inc.

Copyright © 2021 by Daphne Benedis-Grab

All rights reserved. Published by Scholastic Inc., *Publishers since 1920*. SCHOLASTIC and associated logos are trademarks and/or registered trademarks of Scholastic Inc.

The publisher does not have any control over and does not assume any responsibility for author or third-party websites or their content.

Library of Congress Cataloging-in-Publication Data available

ISBN 978-1-338-74633-4

10 9 8 7 6 5 4 3 2   21 22 23 24 25

Printed in the U.S.A.   40

First printing, December 2021

Book design by Maeve Norton

FOR AVI

CHAPTER 1

SUNDAY: 5:30 P.M.
OWEN

It was random that Owen even checked his email before dinner that Sunday. Usually he went straight from pickup basketball with the guys to the backyard. His stepdad, Big Rob, was still insisting it was warm enough for Sunday night barbecues. Which was fine with Owen—give him a pile of ribs soaked in Big Rob's secret Lexington sauce and he would be happy eating outside in January. But Mom said barbecue season in upstate New York ended with the first frost—which had been that morning.

So when Owen got home, Big Rob was standing next to the cold grill, saying, "It was more a light dusting of rain, not an actual frost," while Mom countered that rain did not leave a white icy residue.

Owen figured it would be a while before the family ate anything, so he went into Mom's office to use the computer. His older sister, Jade (who was technically his stepsister), normally hogged it, but Jade was on a college tour with her mom and away for the week. So the computer was free for Owen and the project he had started during the Covid-19 shutdown.

It wasn't something he had told anyone—right now it was just his. But Owen was creating a graphic novel. None of his friends were into comics, drawing, or writing, and while Big Rob was enthused about most of Owen's interests, Mom and Dad were more invested in Owen's grades, which were somewhat less than great. They didn't nag him much, but Owen knew they might butt in if they realized that half the time they thought Owen was doing homework, he was actually working on his story.

Owen had reached a point in the book where he needed to know a little more about the armor worn by samurai for when his character went back in time. He did a quick search, found some great images, and then, while they were printing, logged into his account.

And that was how he ended up being the first of the four to see the email.

GEMMA

"Can I please be excused?" Gemma asked, doing her best to appear casual. This was hard because she was pretty much crawling out of her skin. But it was essential that Mom not see how desperate Gemma was to get on her phone after Mom's new "screen-free Sundays." Mom was still scarred by all the screen time Gemma, Kate, and Avi had had during the Covid-19 shutdown. Although it'd been necessary for school and to socialize online, now that things were open again and people could go out, Gemma's mom was determined to keep them off screens as much as possible.

"Isn't it your night to load the dishwasher?" Gemma's evil younger sister, Kate, asked.

"No, it's Avi's," Gemma said between gritted teeth. Her older brother, who was as sweet as Kate was evil, nodded cheerfully.

"Okay, then," Mom said, sounding reluctant.

"I did all my homework," Gemma said, smiling like she wasn't aching to snatch her phone out of the charging cabinet and fly up to her room.

"Great, off you go," Dad said, waving Gemma toward the living room.

It took everything in her but she managed to walk calmly to the cabinet, take out the phone without checking it (Mom was watching), and meander to the stairs. She didn't start running until she was half-way up and Kate had started moaning about how she hated her math teacher.

And after all that? *He* hadn't even texted.

Gemma threw herself down on her pink comforter-covered bed (so immature, but Mom wouldn't get her a new one until high school, which was years away) and scrolled through her notifications, then went to her inbox. She noticed the email right away and not because the subject line was all caps. Gemma noticed it right away because of what it said.

I KNOW YOUR SECRET

TODD

Todd wanted to punch the computer screen.

He could imagine how it would feel to put his fist through the screen, blasting that email apart—but obviously he didn't. Mom was so proud of the old desktop her boss had given her that it sat in a place of honor on the kitchen table where they ate. Todd knew Mom's boss just wanted to get rid of the computer without hassle since it was ancient, but the important thing was that Mom didn't know that. And it did still work. Even though it took up half the small table in their very small trailer.

"I forgot my milk," Mom said, coming out of her bedroom. She was getting ready to watch her Sunday shows.

Todd quickly closed the email before she could see what was on the screen.

"You know how it helps me relax." She was wearing what she called her "cozy robe," her feet in the bunny slippers Todd had gotten her for her birthday. Mom loved bunnies and wore the slippers every night.

"Want me to get it for you?" Todd asked. He started

to stand up and found he felt shaky, almost dizzy, from what he'd just read.

"No, you keep doing your work on the computer," Mom said, grabbing a teacup and saucer for her milk. It was the "little touches," as she called them, that made Mom happy. That and anything involving bunnies, Todd, or chocolate.

As soon as Mom was safely back in her room, Todd clicked back to the email. As he read it a second time, his fists clenched up.

But punching wasn't going to help him get out of this:

> I know your secret. Do what I say, when I say it, and I won't tell a soul. Skip even one step and I will tell everyone. Text me at this number as soon as you read this email. And then get ready for tomorrow. It's going to be a very big day.

8:12 P.M.
ALLY

Ally's hands were shaking, her breath coming in short, sharp bursts as she shoved things around on her desk, trying to find her phone so she could send the text. Thank goodness she had checked her email tonight! It had been a long day helping Grandpa and Gram— Sundays were always long days, not that Ally minded. Nothing mattered more to her than the animals at the sanctuary she helped her grandparents run. And nothing made her, or her grandparents, happier.

But still, the work was tiring. Often after evening animal feeding and cuddles, Ally took a long, hot shower, fell into bed with a book, and passed out by nine. And what if she had done that tonight and missed this email?

It was too awful to even contemplate.

She finally found her phone, wedged into a far corner of the desk under a pile of *Cat Care* magazines. It took two tries to open up a new message and type in the phone number from the email. Then she hesitated. What was the proper response when someone was blackmailing you? She settled on *It's Ally* and pressed send. Then she waited, cold sweat slithering down her sides, staring at her phone.

Ally had no idea who could be threatening her like this. And how had they found out her secret? It was most certainly the one thing Ally never, ever wanted anyone to know. Because if anyone found out what she had done—

Her stomach tumbled ominously as a bubble appeared on the screen, three dots flashing. Ally closed her eyes and said a quick prayer. This person—whoever they were—had the power to ruin everything Ally had ever truly loved.

CHAPTER 2

MONDAY: 12:50 P.M.

RECORDING PART 1

OWEN: Hi, it's Owen, wait, is this thing even on? [*Muffled thumping sounds.*] Okay, relax, I've got it. So yeah, hello future us, this is Owen and I'm starting this off. What is this? you might ask. And who are we?

ALLY: No one is asking that—we know who we are.

OWEN: Okay, right. Well, we're making this recording to understand why we're doing all this stuff and who is blackmailing us and making us do it. We figure if we go over everything, record it, and then listen to it, maybe we can see something we didn't notice the first time around. That's what our English teacher said happens if you talk something through, step by step. We need to find the clues we missed. Hold up, no one told me Todd had chips—can I get some of those? [*Loud crunch.*]

9

GEMMA: I'm taking over because we need to run through everything that happened today—not get distracted by chips. So first: We all got emails last night telling us to text the blackmailer and await further instructions. Which we all did. And the reply from "Anonymous" said, "Tomorrow morning, go to homeroom for attendance. Next, go to your assigned Explorer's group and tell the teacher you were switched. Then go inside the janitor's closet by the gym and wait for my instructions."

ALLY: That really sucked because I love Explorer's Day and I was in pickle making.

OWEN: [*Indistinctly.*] Gross!

GEMMA: What's gross is you talking with your mouth full.

ALLY: [*Quietly.*] What's wrong with pickles? Everyone likes pickles.

TODD: Ally's right, pickles are awesome. Anyway, we should also mention that the email was made to look like we sent it to ourselves.

GEMMA: I asked my older brother and he says that's a pretty simple hack.

ALLY: So a computer person could figure out the real sender?

OWEN: Yeah, probably. Remember that whole workshop we had in the library about how everyone has a digital footprint and anything you post can be traced back to you eventually? Which means an expert could figure out the anonymous person we're texting too.

GEMMA: Are any of you experts? I'm definitely not.

[*Silence.*]

GEMMA: Since none of us are at that level, we'd have to ask someone to help us and I'm not sure we want anyone seeing these texts.

[*Silence.*]

TODD: Okay, we don't know who's behind this and we're not going to be able to figure it out from the email address and texts. So let's move on to what happened next.

MONDAY: 5:00 A.M.
ALLY

Ally had barely slept after getting the response to her text. Questions gnawed at her: Who was sending these texts? What was she going to be asked to do? Why had she been selected for this? And most of all, how had this person found out Ally's secret, the one thing she was desperate to hide?

She'd barely closed her eyes when the alarm woke her up at five. Groaning, she pushed off the cozy quilt her Aunt Ainyr had made for her and given her parents the day they adopted Ally from Kazakhstan. It had kept Ally warm on some very awful nights. Three years ago Mom and Dad died in a car crash and Ally (and the quilt) had moved from their apartment in Philadelphia to the small town in upstate New York where Gram and Grandpa ran their animal sanctuary. Adjusting to life in Snow Valley had been tough, but Lane Animal Sanctuary felt like home the first time Ally walked into the Cat Corral. The huge room that led to an expansive outdoor area for the rescued cats was a little bit of paradise, despite the hissing and yowling fights its residents got into from time to time.

Ally threw on jeans, a clean t-shirt, and a kind-of-clean sweatshirt, then headed downstairs. Grandpa, the family chef, was tending a pan of crackling sausages on the stove and making sure the toast didn't burn.

"Morning, love," he said to Ally.

She grabbed a plate from the drainer and headed over to Grandpa for her serving of sausage and a morning hug and kiss. Her grandparents were affectionate with both people and animals, which was probably why they were so good at nurturing abused, terrified creatures and, more often than not, helping them become loving pets.

"Cat Corral, the Bark House, or Den of Rabbits?" Grandpa asked as Ally ate. She didn't exactly have an appetite the way her stomach was frothing with anxiety about school, but people who worked with animals could not afford to go out with an empty belly. Food was energy and so it was required.

"Dogs today," Ally said. The three of them split morning feeding, which was one-quarter opening cans and pouring kibble, three-quarters snuggling with animals. And today Ally needed the kind of big snuggles and playing that came at the Bark House.

A chorus of joyful woofing, along with a number of scampering pups, greeted Ally when she entered the Bark House. She knelt down to cuddle Chester, a black-and-brown mix, then scratched Kiki on her fat gray tummy. Waiting behind them were Fozzie, Crackers, and Flash. Ally took her time hugging, patting, and talking to all of them. Buttons came up next, her big brown eyes dancing. Ally gently rubbed her soft ears. The little dog had been painfully thin when she first arrived, her eyes darkened by hopelessness. She'd become a frisky, happy, loving dog in her time at Lane Sanctuary and Ally reminded herself that nothing mattered more than that. *Nothing.*

Ally called greetings to the dogs who were still learning to trust people, then headed to the food closet.

After making sure every dog had breakfast, fresh water, and a lot more hugs, Ally headed for the school bus stop at the end of her driveway. She had to run the last section of the long, winding drive, but she made it just as the bus was about to pull away.

Ally always sat alone on the bus to school. She

didn't have friends in Snow Valley, which was such a small town that the middle and high schools shared the same building. Everyone had grown up together and formed friendships long before Ally showed up in fourth grade. Not like she would have had time for friends anyway. Ally spent every hour she wasn't required to be at school working with Grandpa and Gram at the sanctuary. The sanctuary was her life, it was her heart, it was the thing that mattered most.

Which was why today Ally had to do whatever this blackmailer told her to do. Because if she didn't and her secret got out? Lane Animal Sanctuary would close for good.

TODD

No one talked to Todd as he walked up the path to the steps of Snow Valley Secondary School. Groups of friends hung out on the big lawn and congregated under trees. The high schoolers lounged on the prize seating, the wide staircase. None of them bothered with Todd though, which was just how he liked it. Especially today. Because right now, if anyone even looked at him funny, it was possible Todd would explode. Not on purpose exactly, but when there was this much lava burning and churning in his gut, he sometimes erupted and that never went well. It was also probably the reason most people at school stayed out of his way.

Todd had gotten a reputation for hitting people back in kindergarten and by seventh grade everyone knew to avoid him. Sure, he hadn't hit anyone in a long time—but that was because he hadn't had to.

He'd only lost it once this year—when Owen and Cody came into Todd's locker alcove. Cody was making annoying jokes, like he was trying to impress Owen. Which seemed like a waste of time to Todd—who cared what an idiot like Owen thought? But then Cody said, "Todd got the lowest score on the quiz again, because he's the dumbest kid in the school," and what was Todd supposed to do, ignore him? Act like he didn't care? Todd did care. His quiz score was low because he hadn't been able to study—Mom had been in one of her moods where she came home crying from work every day. Those were the times Todd needed to take care of things, make sure that the trailer was clean, that the bills were paid on time, that Mom got her milk in her cup with the saucer every night. So no, he hadn't aced that math quiz but he'd aced plenty of other quizzes and he was *not* the dumbest kid in school. The dumbest kid in school was obviously Cody because (a) he'd said that in front of Todd and (b) he was surprised when Todd punched him. The whole thing had been a big mess with Principal Grace but Todd managed to keep Mom from learning about his suspension (he'd long ago perfected her signature and was always home in time to erase upsetting voicemails), which was all that mattered.

Todd tossed his coat into his locker and slammed it shut with a satisfying thunk, letting out some of his anger. He hated that some clown was threatening him, making him do stuff he didn't want to do (he had no idea what he'd be asked to do, but he knew he wouldn't want to do it). But what choice did he have? If his secret came out he would be in major trouble. Mom would shatter like one of her delicate teacups, and what would happen then?

Todd stomped into his homeroom and threw himself in his seat, sending a glare around the room. No one met his gaze. In fact, the snobby girl who sat in front of him, Gemma, moved her chair farther away from him. Before Todd could decide whether to say something nasty about this, Mr. Patel walked in and cheerfully greeted his homeroom. Mr. Patel was cheerful every day. He was also kind and always went out of his way to ask Todd about Mom, who he'd met at the store. Todd wasn't someone who actually liked teachers, obviously. But Mr. Patel was okay.

"I bet all of you are as excited about Explorer's Day as I am!" Mr. Patel said, setting down his take-out cup from the Snow Valley Diner.

Of course he was extra cheerful today. Though honestly, Todd did generally enjoy Explorer's Day. There were two a year, and students got to take immersion classes in fun things like board games and cake baking. Last time Todd had been in ice cream where they learned about the history of ice cream, and then got to make any flavor they could dream up. Todd had created an incredible mix of chocolate crunchies, pretzels, crushed peanut butter cups, and mini marshmallows in a mocha-caramel ice cream blend. He and Mom had eaten it for dinner that night and Mom had said it was the best ice cream she'd ever had. Today Todd was supposed to be in puzzle mania and that would have been really cool if he'd been able to go. Which he couldn't. And now his anger flared up again.

Morning announcements came on over the scratchy loudspeaker, a list of clubs Todd couldn't join because he had to get home right after school every day, a list of sports happening over the weekend that Todd would not go see, and then a long rant from Principal Grace about bullying. The school had started a big zero-tolerance campaign around bullying a few weeks ago and Todd was sick of hearing about it. Next was an announcement for upcoming play tryouts that got Gemma so excited he could see her bounce slightly in her seat, and finally the principal signed off.

Mr. Patel called roll and then clapped his hands together with delight. "Okay, everyone, enjoy your explorations! Come check in if you're not sure what classroom to go to. And I'll see all of you at the wrap-up assembly this afternoon."

Explorer groups spent the morning and early afternoon working on projects that were then displayed at the Showcases set up in the gym. The best were food exhibits because there were samples—last year Todd had managed to visit the candy-making table twice—but even things like quilting and songwriting could be cool. The final part of the day was an assembly with a big slide show of pictures from the day, and a rep from each group coming up to share stories from their "process." Todd wasn't going to admit it, but seeing a photo of himself in last year's ice cream group putting whipped cream on his creation had been nice. But obviously nothing nice would be happening this year.

Todd hustled out of the classroom and joined the crowd of people in the hall. Everyone was excited, heading off for a fun day. Everyone but Todd.

Someone came up too close behind Todd and stepped on his heel.

Todd whirled around, furious, and saw that it was Kirby, looking completely panicked. "Sorry," he said, glancing side to side like he might need an escape plan. Then he ducked his head and scurried off.

"No problem," Todd said as Kirby disappeared around the corner. Last year Todd had overheard Kirby calling him "a walking anger management problem." Todd had handled this by punching Kirby, which might have proven Kirby's point, but did shut him up. And clearly Kirby had not forgotten it, though his reaction just now seemed a little over the top. That incident had been a pretty long time ago.

"No pushing," Vivi said irritably. She was walking past Todd, and a group of boys were trying to get by her. Vivi was the class snitch, always ordering people around and telling on them when they didn't do as she said. She and Todd had had a number of run-ins and now, as she held up her arm to stop the boys, Todd glared at her.

"Move," he snapped.

She glared back but did lower her arm out of Todd's way.

Satisfied, Todd continued to room 106 where puzzle mania was being held and, per his instructions from the blackmailer, told Ms. Nguyen, the teacher in charge, that he had been switched to bread baking. And now that he had his official reason for not being present, he made his way past the cafeteria and toward the janitor's closet—step three from the blackmailer. Normally something like that would never work, but no one was paying attention to Todd. The blackmailer had picked a good day for this—Explorer's Day was always hectic.

The closet was right outside the cafeteria doors. Like half the hallway, it was papered with an anti-bullying poster. Todd glanced around casually. No one was looking. He opened the door, which had an alarmingly sticky handle, and stepped inside. Then stopped.

Because something very unexpected had happened. Unexpected and unwelcome.

Someone was in the closet.

OWEN

Owen nearly shrieked in surprise when the door to the closet opened. A shadowy figure stepped in and Owen cringed, his mind racing as he tried to come up with a reason he could explain to the janitor why he was standing here next to the utility sink. Or was this the blackmailer, coming to threaten Owen in person?

But then the person spoke and it was not the janitor. "Beat it," Todd said. Which was not what the blackmailer would say, so now Owen had a different problem on his hands. Todd was not someone to tangle with—Owen had seen him fight up close—but he couldn't just leave. Given the power the blackmailer had over Owen, the choice was clear: He was going to have to stand up to Todd.

But before he could say anything, another person shoved the closet door open.

Todd jumped in surprise as Gemma slid inside and closed the door behind her.

"What are you guys doing in here?" she demanded, crossing her arms over her chest. Her face was pinched and her voice was sharp. Gemma was the only seventh-grade starter on the girls JV basketball team and not someone to mess with.

"None of your business," Todd said, crossing his own arms over his chest.

"Well, get out. I have a call to make and I need privacy," Gemma said as Todd moved to stand next to the mop rack. The closet reeked of overly zesty pine cleaner that was starting to make Owen's eyes water.

"Find somewhere else to make it," Todd snapped. "I was here first."

"Actually, *I* was here first," Owen said.

"So—" Gemma started, but then she stumbled forward. The closet door had opened again, hitting into her and letting in yet another person. This time it was a short, quiet girl who was in Owen's gym class. He was pretty sure her name was Alice.

Alice stepped in and looked around at the three of them. "Oh, are you guys being blackmailed too?" she asked.

For a moment Owen stiffened and he saw Gemma press her lips together and Todd clench his fists. Which was when Owen knew Alice was right—they were all here for the same reason.

"Yeah," he said, leaning back on the utility sink, "I am."

Gemma sighed. "Me too."

They all looked at Todd, who shrugged, then nodded.

"Well, then," Alice said. "I have instructions to text the blackmailer once I'm here."

"Me too," Owen said, and Todd and Gemma nodded.

"I don't know about you guys but I'm doing everything I'm told, no questions asked," Alice added.

"Same. I suggest we don't ask each other any questions either," Gemma said, getting out her phone to text the blackmailer.

They pretty much all fell over each other agreeing to that.

Once the texts had been sent, they waited, phones in hand.

"What's taking so long?" Todd muttered.

Alice looked up. "I think it's been, like, a minute." She had a calm way of speaking that Owen found soothing. As much as anything could be soothing when you were stuck in a pine-saturated closet with three people you barely knew, waiting to hear from a blackmailer.

"I wasn't asking you," Todd snapped. "Do you even go to school here?"

Alice slumped. "Yeah, I'm in your math class. Last year I was in your social studies and science classes. I'm Ally."

Ally, whoops. Well, Owen had been close.

Todd looked at his screen for a second, and then said something that shocked Owen. "Sorry, I recognize you now. I just want to know what this person is going to make us do and I hate waiting."

Ally nodded. "I get it, believe me." She leaned against the wall by the sink and tucked her hands into her pockets.

The closet was large for a closet but still a pretty tight space and it had a fair amount of cleaning supplies stuffed into it. Across from the big square sink was a wall rack of industrial mops and brooms, and the back wall had shelves with bottles, cans, and sponges. There was also a big metal mop bucket that poked out from under the sink and Owen noted it would be easy to walk into it if you weren't looking.

"Do you guys have any idea who's sending us these messages?" Owen asked. He'd been thinking about it all morning but still had no idea himself.

"And why the four of us?" Ally added. This was another good question that Owen could not make sense of.

"How does this person know stuff that's secret?" Gemma asked. "Are they some kind of stalker?"

"And what are they going to tell us to do?" Todd asked, kicking at the metal mop bucket.

That was when their phones all vibrated.

GEMMA

> I just put a bag under the back right side dumpster behind the cafeteria. Go to the dumpster shed, get the bag, then come back to the closet and text me. You have ten minutes to complete this task. Clock's ticking.

"Is everyone else going dumpster-diving?" Owen asked cheerfully.

Gemma and the others nodded. Gemma had never been a fan of Owen, who was like a big, goofy puppy, making dumb jokes and messing around with his friends. Yes, it was typical of boys their age but so unsophisticated. And so unlike Miles.

"Is this really going to take four of us?" Todd asked.

Gemma thought he might have a point. Maybe she could stay here while one of them went to grab it. But Ally was nodding. "One of us has to keep watch at the door, one of us has to keep watch at the dumpster, and it might take two of us to carry back whatever it is we're getting."

Unfortunately that made sense.

"Let's do it," Owen said, like they were off to the movies, not going to muck around under a dumpster, something guaranteed to be disgusting.

Ally opened the door very slowly, very quietly, then peered out. "All clear," she said softly. Gemma didn't know Ally at all but she was glad Ally was part of the group—she was obviously cautious and thoughtful, unlike the other two people they were stuck with.

Gemma, Todd, and Owen followed Ally out into the empty hallway papered with club notices, anti-bullying posters, and a big sign about Explorer's Day. They tip-toed past the large display featuring the New York State

Gold Star Award plaque and certificate. The award was given out once a year to a school that "excelled in academics, community involvement, and student life" but the trophy just reminded Gemma of the achingly boring assembly last spring when the award had been presented to Principal Grace, who was now constantly pushing the school to "continue to excel" in hopes of winning it a second year in a row. Despite how annoying that was, Gemma *was* thankful for the award because it had resulted in a lot of donations from parents, several to the theater department, which meant this year's play was going to include both the middle and high schools. Gemma was a huge fan of anything that mixed together middle and high school students.

Just then the door of the main office opened and Gemma froze, her heart slamming hard into her ribs. Luckily it was just a high school student who walked out, a senior named Dana. Gemma had seen her there when she'd gone in for a late pass last week—Dana was getting volunteer hours helping out the administrative assistant, Ms. Atkins.

Dana hadn't been friendly to Gemma when she'd gone to the office, but that was nothing compared with the poisonous look she gave Owen as she passed.

"Someone hates you," Todd noted, somewhat happily, after Dana had gone up the stairs to the high school.

Owen shook his head and frowned. "Yeah, I used to be friends with her brother and I accidentally gave him strawberry jam at my house, not knowing he has a berry allergy. He was fine but Dana still acts like I tried to kill him. Their whole family holds grudges."

Gemma was on Dana's side here—allergies were serious and it sounded like Owen had been an idiot.

"Who's her brother?" Ally asked.

"That kid Cody," Todd said, scowling. "He's the worst."

"You shouldn't be mean about him," Gemma said. "He left school two weeks ago to go to boarding school because he was getting bullied here."

"That's so awful," Ally said, clearly surprised. Gemma felt bad for her—*everyone* knew about Cody leaving to go to some school in Virginia. Or maybe it was Maryland. But in any case it was far away and everyone, except apparently Ally, knew about it.

But while Ally might not have been on top of school gossip, she was a good lookout. She peeked around the corner, then led them to the exit off the school kitchen.

None of the cafeteria workers had arrived yet so it was eerily quiet as they walked through.

"I can hold the door and keep lookout unless someone else wants to," Ally said when they got there. "I'll just say I'm here for my Explorer's class."

Obviously Gemma had hoped for that job but she'd look like a brat if she argued, so she said, "Sure," and headed out back with the boys.

The dumpster shed, which was really more of an enclosure, was surprisingly clean. Even the cement under Gemma's black flats was scrubbed and smelled fresh. That is, it smelled fresh until they arrived at the back dumpster on the right and headed for the far corner. It was the most neglected dumpster because while the inside was clear of gross things, it reeked of rotten fruit, old meat, and something that had been molding for a long, long time.

"This is disgusting," Gemma said. She did not even want to think what awaited them under this thing where garbage went to die.

"What did you expect?" Todd asked scornfully.

But Todd was a known jerk so, really, his attitude was to be expected. "If you're so comfortable, why don't you see what's under there?" Gemma asked sweetly.

Owen snickered and Todd whipped around to glare at him. "Something funny?" he asked.

"No, I just—" Owen stammered, his face going a bit pink, probably more from surprise than anything else. Todd's temper really went from zero to one hundred fast. No wonder everyone in school avoided him.

"What?" Todd demanded, taking a step toward Owen.

This would not do. The clock was ticking and the last thing they needed was to get caught out here because these two immature idiots got in a fight. "Stop talking, both of you," Gemma said in the voice that could even quiet her evil sister, Kate. "I'll do it. Just keep watch so no one sees us."

"I can do it, really," Owen said, all eager.

But Gemma didn't trust him to handle this properly—he seemed like the kind of person who was sloppy with details. And considering what was at risk if Gemma's secret got out? No way was she taking chances.

"I've got it," she informed him, then headed over to the far corner of the dumpster. She knelt down to get the lay of the land before rooting around. This was clearly the hardest place to clean, which was why garbage remnants were shoved under the dumpster wheels. There wasn't anything rotting, despite the smell—it was more plastic bags and plastic utensils. Gemma bent down fully so she could see underneath the dumpster, glad she had worn skinny jeans today instead of a skirt.

It took her eyes a moment to adjust to the dim light but then she saw that among the empties was a bag that clearly had something stuffed into it. This had to be what the blackmailer wanted them to find.

Gemma put one hand—a hand that she would wash very thoroughly—on the side of the dumpster for balance as she reached her other arm under the corner, feeling around for the full bag. Her fingers first landed on something sticky and she bit back a groan. But it had to be done so she reached farther underneath the dumpster until her hand touched the full, and thankfully not sticky, bag. She pulled it out carefully, then stood up and, holding the bag a safe distance from her sweater, walked over to the boys.

"I've got it," she said.

"Awesome!" Owen said, like Gemma had just scored a touchdown.

"Are you sure that's the right thing?" Todd asked in a skeptical voice.

"Feel free to check yourself if you don't believe me," Gemma said, trying to sound soothing, the way Ally spoke, and not irritated by Todd, which was how she was actually feeling.

"What's inside?" Owen asked, coming to walk next to Gemma as she headed to the open cafeteria door where Ally was waiting.

"I don't know," Gemma said, "and we don't want to waste time looking right now—we have to get back and text the blackmailer before nine or we'll be over our ten-minute limit." And to be honest, she didn't want to touch the bag any more than she had to.

"She's right, let's get going," Todd agreed, from behind.

Which was the first non-rude thing he had said to Gemma.

"Got it," she told Ally when they reached the door.

"Nice job," Ally said. "I'll go first to make sure the coast is clear, since you guys did the dirty work."

"One of us did," Gemma muttered as Ally led the way back through the silent kitchen, through the cafeteria, down the hall, and back to the janitor's closet.

Once inside, the other three immediately took out their phones and texted the anonymous number, while Gemma went right to the utility sink to scrub her hands.

"So what's in the bag?" Owen asked, nearly pushing into Gemma in his eagerness. She could smell the cereal he'd eaten for breakfast on his breath, something fruity and sweet. It was gross.

Gemma kicked the bag toward him. It was the size of the plastic bags her family used in their kitchen trash can and was nearly full. "You can do the honors," she told him.

She was curious, of course, but after her brush with the dumpster she was done handling disgusting things.

Owen slowly untied the plastic ties holding it closed. He bent to look inside, then straightened up fast, his nose wrinkled up. "It's a bunch of clothes and it stinks."

"What kind of clothes?" Ally asked.

"Who cares?" Todd asked.

"It might tell us something about the person we're texting," Ally explained.

Todd nodded. "Yeah, okay, that makes sense."

Gemma had to admit she was impressed with how Ally handled Todd. He was nicer to her than she'd ever seen him be to anyone.

Owen peered back in the bag, then reached inside, moving the contents around.

"Don't take anything out," Gemma said quickly. She had no idea why the blackmailer wanted this bag but she wouldn't risk them messing it up or losing one of the items inside.

"I won't," Todd said. "Okay, so there's jeans, a sweatshirt, and"—he paused for a second—"oh, gross, underwear." With that he stood up and closed the bag.

"Boy or girl underwear?" Ally asked.

"Boy," Owen said, his nose still scrunched. "Used."

They all groaned a little at that.

And then their phones vibrated.

CHAPTER 3

MONDAY: 12:54 P.M.

RECORDING PART 2

GEMMA: So we went down the hall and saw Dana—she holds grudges and hates Owen—

OWEN: Hey, that's not a detail we need!

GEMMA: We need *every* detail—that's the point. Which brings me to my next question—Owen, do you remember anything about the clothes? Or if there was anything else in the bag?

OWEN: [*Slight moan.*] So not what I want to remember, but okay. There were jeans and a sweatshirt, and the other stuff besides the underwear was gym clothes.

TODD: So the blackmailer put dirty clothes under the dumpster—

ALLY: Instead of putting it somewhere less disgusting.

OWEN: Obviously the blackmailer hates us so he or she put it in the grimiest place possible, just to make our lives harder.

GEMMA: *My* life harder—you just stood around while I did the dirty work.

ALLY: The point is, these pieces are all part of a bigger plan—and we have to figure out what that plan is before it explodes in our faces.

MONDAY: 8:51 A.M.
OWEN

Go together to locker A-18. Bring the bag of clothes. You have ten minutes to get there and text me. Go.

"That's it?" Owen asked. "Just go to the locker with the clothes?"

"I'm sure there'll be more instructions when we get there," Gemma said in a tone Owen was starting to notice she only used with him. It was the sort of tone

Owen's Aunt Sam used with her twin toddlers, Dash and Shiloh. Clearly Gemma thought Owen had the mental capacity of a three-year-old.

"We could get in a lot of trouble standing around a locker alcove on our phones," Owen said, trying to sound mature and serious. Unfortunately he burped right after, making Ally snicker and Gemma scowl.

"Like the blackmailer cares if we get in trouble," Todd said, rolling his eyes. Great, now Todd was talking to him like he was a toddler too.

"I think what Owen's saying is that we need a plan so we don't get caught," Ally said, giving him a slight smile.

Owen smiled back. Ally was so nice. Which had Owen curious—what could she possibly have to hide? Todd probably had a million secrets that would get him in big trouble if they came out, and Gemma—well, he could see her hiding *something*. But Ally, who seemed so honest and sincere? It was impossible to imagine her doing something so awful she'd go along with being blackmailed to keep it hidden.

"Good thinking," Gemma said to Ally. "But we have to come up with it fast—we're already down to nine minutes."

"One of us needs to be the lookout," Ally said.

"You should do it," Todd said, just as Owen was about to volunteer for the job. He felt the experience of being a real-life lookout would allow him to make the crucial stakeout scene in his graphic novel even more realistic. "You did a good job when we were at the dumpster."

"Thanks and, sure, I'd be happy to," Ally said, sounding pleased.

"Okay, and what's our excuse if a teacher sees us in the hall?" Gemma asked. Owen noticed her peeking at her phone. They wouldn't get another blackmail text until they reached the locker but she must be nervous.

Unless the phone had something to do with her secret. Not that he would ask—he certainly didn't want anyone digging into what he himself had to hide.

"Um, our immersion teacher sent us to the office for something?" Ally suggested hesitantly, brushing at a lock of hair that had fallen out of her sloppy pony-tail. It was kind of funny how Ally looked like she had rolled out of bed and put on her father's clothes while Gemma looked ready for a photo shoot.

"No way a teacher would send all four of us," Todd said. He turned to Owen. "Do you have any ideas?" he asked with a sneer.

Todd's secret probably involved a buried body.

Possibly more than one. But as it happened, Owen *did* have an idea.

"We say we're in the comic book immersion and we forgot some of the supplies we were supposed to bring, so Ms. Lydon told us to go to our lockers to get them," Owen said.

"Would we need supplies for that immersion?" Gemma asked Ally, like she didn't trust Owen to know the answer.

"Yes," Owen said, so loudly that the other three shushed him. "That was my immersion, and if we had any comics we'd made or special drawing tools, we were supposed to bring them."

"You draw comics?" Todd asked skeptically.

"I'm making a graphic novel and it's good," Owen said, the words just coming out. But he wasn't going to let Todd make his graphic novel a joke. He didn't mind Todd mocking him about stuff that didn't matter, but this did.

Todd considered this, then nodded. "Cool," he said, and Owen nearly fell over from shock.

"That's actually a good excuse, then," Gemma said. Owen tried to ignore how surprised she sounded that he'd come up with a decent idea. "And we need to get going—we're down to seven minutes."

Ally opened the door a sliver and Owen, clothes bag in hand, stepped forward, ready for her signal to head out.

But instead Ally shut the door, turned, her eyes wide, and gestured frantically that they needed to be quiet. Owen sucked in his breath for fear of making the tiniest noise as footsteps sounded in the hall outside, then stopped right in front of the closet door.

GEMMA

Gemma was holding her breath and she was pretty sure everyone else was as well. The hall outside was silent. After what felt like ten minutes, Gemma had to suck in some air. There was still no sound outside in the hall. They were trapped and the clock was ticking. What if the person outside was Mr. Wilton or Mr. Smith, the two janitors who worked on the middle school floors? How could the four of them possibly explain hanging out in a closet of cleaning supplies during Explorer's Day? Whatever lie they came up with, there was no way they'd make it to locker A-18 in time. And the thought of missing the deadline given by the blackmailer had Gemma feeling like she'd swallowed a handful of sand.

Ally had an ear pressed against the door, Todd's fists were curled (like hitting something would help), and Owen's pinkish complexion was turning chalky. Cleary they were as anxious as Gemma about their secrets being revealed.

"Yes, but I have to help with it," a woman said, right in front of the door. The voice was familiar but Gemma could not quite place it. And now there was silence—clearly this person was on a phone. Gemma was momentarily distracted by how unfair it was that teachers could use their phones in school but students got theirs confiscated.

It felt like an hour passed with the person just standing there, listening to someone on the other end of the phone. Gemma pressed her hands together. How long were they going to be stuck here, waiting? She was starting to feel itchy all over, like her skin didn't fit right. And the pine smell was an assault on her senses. Why wouldn't the person leave already?! And why was it so hot in here? Gemma was boiling!

The person spoke again.

"Right, that was the agreement when I was hired but then the school got the Gold Star Award, the first one given out after the Covid-19 closings, and he was in the papers and turned into a local hero. What principal is retiring after that?"

Ally was staring wide-eyed at the door, as if she could see through to Ms. Montenegro, the assistant principal, whose voice Gemma now recognized. Owen also looked shocked to hear a member of the administration gossiping like this, while Todd just grinned.

Gemma herself was somewhere in between, scandalized but also kind of amused. Though she was mostly eager for Ms. Montenegro to move already.

"No, he's working to get us the award again this year, and if he gets it for the school twice in a row he'll probably never leave," Ms. Montenegro said. "I know, I was supposed to take over his job this year but now who knows when that will happen?"

And then came the sound of steps walking briskly away from the closet. She was leaving! Gemma was ready to fling the door open and sprint down the hall, but lucky for them, Ally was in charge. She waited until the steps were faint, then cracked open the door and looked out. Then she threw it open and that's when they raced down the hall, coming to a stop at the corner. Ally peeked around, then nodded, and they were flying again.

They were all panting when they arrived at the A locker alcove. Each alcove was wrapped around a pillar, giving it three sides, and Gemma hurried to check around both corners to make sure no one was there. Then she sent her text, the others quickly following. They'd texted with a minute and three seconds to spare. Gemma leaned against the lockers and let out her first breath in the past nine minutes.

"That was close," Ally said, sliding her ancient phone into her baggy jeans pocket and positioning herself to keep watch. Gemma respected a girl's right to choose her own style but it was hard to understand why Ally opted for baggy clothes in unflattering colors that made her look like a farmhand. *Not* that she was judging. Gemma firmly believed girls needed to be allies and build each other up, not tear each other down. So if Ally wanted to dress like a farmhand, Gemma was supportive. Confused, but supportive.

"Too close," Owen said, crouching down to a squat.

His face still looked pasty. What had Owen done that would make him go along with this? And have him this worried? Gemma decided it was probably a mistake he'd made, something thoughtless that would have bad consequences. Todd was pacing the back of the alcove. It was easy to think of twenty things he might have done, needless to say. The big mystery was Ally, who was now twisting the end of her ponytail. What could someone who seemed so nice and honest, like she'd just stepped out of a family sitcom, do to be in trouble like this?

And then Gemma's phone, which was still clenched in her hand, vibrated with a text.

TODD

> Open the locker. 10-17-38. Put the bag of clothes inside. Close the locker. Return to the closet. You have ten minutes. Go.

"Wait, we're supposed to break into someone's locker?" Ally asked, sounding anxious.

"Yes," Todd said, pushing past Owen to get to A-18.

They only had ten minutes and after the near disaster of coming to the locker alcove so late, Todd was not interested in wasting a second of their time.

"We could get in real trouble for that," Owen said, sounding just as anxious as Ally. "Maybe we should think about this a second."

"There's nothing to think about," Todd said, spinning the combination lock. He hit the 10 but went past 17 because his hands were shaking, a sign the volcano was starting in his gut.

"Maybe we could tie the bag to the locker so the person gets the clothes but not actually break into it?" Gemma asked hesitantly.

"No, the blackmailer said we have to follow their directions exactly," Todd said, his teeth gritted as he missed 10 this time. "Tying the bag to the locker is not what they said to do."

"I think he's right," Owen said as Todd began spinning the lock a third time. "But we should—"

"Stop talking!" Todd shouted, punching the locker. "If we don't do this, that blackmailing maniac is going to ruin my life!"

There was silence. Todd clenched his fists, trying

to get his hands to stop shaking and his breath to slow. But the lava was starting to boil as the pressure built inside him.

Then Ally stepped forward. "Keep watch," she told Owen. She walked over and placed a hand on Todd's shoulder. He was about to shake it off when she said, "My life would be ruined too. Everything that matters to me would be decimated. So move."

Todd turned and looked into Ally's eyes. She meant it, he could tell—this was as high-stakes for her as it was for him.

"I've got this," Ally said calmly, and Todd moved.

Ally twirled the dial and the locker popped open. Todd peered in but didn't see anything remarkable—just a messy pile of books and some candy bar wrappers. It actually looked a lot like his locker.

"Give me the clothes," Ally said.

Owen, who usually had something to say about everything, silently tossed over the bag from where he was keeping watch.

Ally set it inside the locker, then closed the door, spun the lock, and brushed off her hands. "Let's get back to the closet," she said.

Todd nodded. Ally was calling the shots now, and all of them knew it.

ALLY

As they walked through the halls, Ally was having a hard time keeping this morning's sausage inside her stomach. Bile was burning its way up her throat and her belly was a bubbling mess. She had never, ever broken a rule in school. She'd never cheated, never been late, never handed in an assignment past the due date, never bullied, never shown up in gym without her gym clothes, and never talked back to a teacher. But now—now Ally was a rule breaker. And not just any rule: It was a crime to break into a locker. That had been made clear at the start of sixth grade. Until six months ago Ally would never have believed herself capable of committing a crime. But as of right now, she had officially committed two.

Gemma was in the lead and she slowed to check around the corner before waving them through. Owen got to the closet first and held the door for all of them. The thick scent of pine made Ally's stomach seethe and she pressed both hands against it, trying to keep from puking. Though at least there was the utility sink if things got bad. Ally walked over next to it, then slid down on the floor, leaned against the cool cement wall, and pulled out her phone to join the others in sending their text.

"I'm not sure how clean that floor is," Gemma said, tucking her phone in her pocket after sending her text and coming to stand next to Ally. "Or that wall."

"We're in a closet of cleaning supplies. I think she's good," Todd pointed out. He was leaning with his back against the door.

"I guess," Gemma said. Then she surprised Ally by sinking down and sitting next to her.

"So whose locker did we just break into?" Owen asked. He was pacing around the small space, which was kind of irritating, but Ally decided not to point it out.

"I don't know," Gemma said, reaching over to brush a piece of lint off one of her shoes. Ally couldn't imagine even noticing something like that—clearly this was why Gemma always looked so put together and Ally did not. "I'm not in A alcove and none of my friends have lockers there either. What about you guys?"

Todd shook his head and reached out a hand to

stop Owen from pacing. "I'm in B and I don't have friends."

There was an awkward silence because while this probably hadn't surprised any of them, it was kind of hard to come up with a response. So Ally decided it would be best to get back on track.

"I'm in C too," she said. She chose not to mention that she also didn't have friends whose lockers she hung out at.

"Oh, where's your locker?" Gemma asked, turning to Ally and seeming pleased to make this discovery.

It would have been nice under other circumstances. "I'm C-47, three lockers down from you," Ally said.

Owen burst out laughing.

Gemma sent him a venomous glare. "Not helpful, Owen. And where's your locker?"

Owen was still grinning but managed to answer. "I'm in D and most of my friends are too, so we mostly meet up there. I don't know if any of them are in A."

"So that's a dead end," Todd said with a sigh. "We have no idea whose locker it is or why someone wanted us to put that bag inside it."

"If we could figure out who's doing this, maybe we could figure out how to make them stop," Ally said.

"That's true, but I have no idea who would put the four of us together or who would want a random bag of clothes put in someone's locker," Gemma said.

Neither did Ally. It made no sense, and yet it was happening.

"Maybe we'll get a clue from the next ask—because this could get a lot worse," Gemma continued.

Ally was chilled by the truth of these words—unless they could figure out who was blackmailing them, they were powerless to stop it. They would just have to keep looking for clues and hope that at some point the blackmailer accidentally revealed themselves.

Owen had stopped grinning. "I hope our next assignment isn't bad because that was super stressful."

Ally nodded along with Gemma and Todd.

Gemma turned to Ally. "But you were so calm out there—I couldn't tell you were stressed at all."

"Yeah, you totally kept it together," Owen agreed. He was looking at Ally carefully, like he could not understand how this was possible.

"I'm good at staying calm," Ally said, hands still pressed to her belly. "You have to be if you work with traumatized animals."

"You work with animals?" Owen asked at the same

time Todd said, "Who's traumatizing animals?"

Todd sounded so angry at the thought that Ally had to smile—his feelings were hers exactly. "My grandparents and I run Lane Animal Sanctuary," she said. "We take in mentally and physically abused animals, and work with them until they're ready for a home with good people who will love them and care for them properly." This was on every flyer and poster about Lane Animal Sanctuary but Ally never got tired of saying it. She was so proud of what they did.

"What happens if they're never ready for real homes?" Owen asked, coming to sit next to Ally on her other side.

"And why are there psychos out there hurting animals?" Todd asked, irritated.

"I don't know. It makes me angry too," Ally told Todd. But she certainly didn't want to talk about her reaction to the people who were unkind to animals so she turned to Owen. "We have a really good rehabilitation rate but there have been a few animals who just couldn't fully recover."

Owen's face paled. "What happened to those animals?"

Ally grinned. "We kept them. Any animal who

makes it to Lane Sanctuary has a home for life, no matter what."

Owen grinned back and nodded. "Awesome."

"How do you work with them so they're ready for new homes?" Gemma asked.

"It depends on the animal," Ally said. "My grandma's kind of an animal whisperer—she says if you listen closely and look carefully, an animal will tell you what they need to heal. So Gramps and I mostly follow her instructions. But certain things are true for every animal—we speak with kindness, we respect their space, we love them, and we always, always stay calm. That way they know we're safe. And that's the first step to learning to trust people again."

It was good to talk about the animals. So good her stomach was settling back down.

"What a cool thing to do," Gemma said.

"What a fun place to live," Owen added. "Getting to play with animals all the time. I love dogs but my stepdad's allergic so we can't have one."

"I always wanted a cat," Todd said quietly.

"Is one of your parents allergic?" Owen asked sympathetically.

"It's just me and my mom and, no, it's not that. It's

just—" Todd paused and his face seemed to close a little. "We don't have time to take care of a pet."

Normally Ally would have pointed out that caring for a cat was not time-consuming and the love that came in return was more than worth it, but something in Todd's face stopped her. He was clearly not saying everything he was thinking. Instead she went back to what Owen had said.

"It's a lot of work to look after the animals, a lot of cleaning and food duty," she told him. "But you're right, it's an amazing place to live." Her voice hardened at the thought that if this day went wrong she might not get to keep living at the sanctuary. She'd be sent to a school for kids who broke the law and the sanctuary would be closed for good.

"So where are your parents?" Owen asked.

"Shut up, Owen," Gemma hissed, leaning around Ally so she could glare at Owen.

"It's okay, they died a long time ago," Ally said. It wasn't okay, of course; Ally would always miss them. But the empty hole of their loss had become more of an ache and less of a gaping wound over time.

"I'm still sorry," Gemma said, patting Ally's knee.

Which was a really kind thing to say. Gemma had

always seemed so polished and popular and above everything. But it turned out she was really nice too.

"Thanks," Ally said softly.

The muffled sound of a phone vibrating made Gemma start and grab for her phone.

"Is it from the blackmailer?" Todd asked, scrambling to get his phone out of his pocket.

"No, just a text about, um, play tryouts," Gemma said, beaming at her screen.

"The play's a big deal this year, isn't it?" Ally asked, happy to move on to a topic that did not involve her life. "There've been a lot of announcements and signs about it."

"It's because of the Gold Star donations," Gemma explained. "Principal Grace requested parents give money for a whole new lighting and sound system—it's top-of-the-line now. And then parents got excited so there's money for costumes and set stuff too."

"I didn't know Principal Grace cared about drama," Ally said. "All he talks about is the Gold Star."

"And bullying," Todd added, rolling his eyes.

"Actually I think those are all connected," Owen said. "My sister is president of the drama club and she said Grace requested it because if the school wins the Gold

Star again, the awards ceremony would be here. And he wants the coverage to be top-quality, like with good sound and lights and stuff, since it will be on the local news. He made sure they got this big spotlight and everything."

"So he got the parents to buy him a spotlight? What an egomaniac," Todd snorted. Ally had to agree—parent donations were supposed to be for students, not to make the principal look good on stage.

"The point is that this year's play will be incredible," Gemma said in a snippy tone. "A spotlight is an important part of the theater."

"You're really into the play," Owen observed.

Gemma scowled, her phone now clutched in her hand. "Is there something wrong with that? I happen to enjoy drama."

Ally was surprised Gemma was so defensive. A lot of students in the middle school were hyped about the play this year.

Owen seemed taken aback as well. "Rehearsals are the same time as basketball practice so you can't do both. Even bench players like me can't miss training and you're a starter."

"I'm not playing basketball this year," Gemma said.

"Are you serious? You're the only seventh-grade starter," Owen said, looking shocked. "If I had your spot, I'd live in the gym."

"Well, I'm not you. The play is way more important to me," Gemma said forcefully.

"My sister talks about everyone in the club," Owen said. "She never mentioned you being there until, like, two weeks ago."

"It's a new interest," Gemma informed him frostily.

Did the drama club have something to do with Gemma's secret? And quitting basketball when you were a starter was a really big deal.

But before Ally could think more about this, all four of their phones vibrated.

CHAPTER 4

RECORDING PART 3

OWEN: So thanks to Ms. Montenegro having that conversation right outside the closet, we were almost late to the locker alcove.

ALLY: I don't even want to know what would have happened if we were. I think the blackmailer is serious about time limits.

OWEN: Agreed. But we made it and then we put the bag in the locker and came back to the closet. I don't think there's anything else to say about that.

GEMMA: Was there anything unusual in the alcove?

TODD: Like what, a secret camera?

ALLY: I don't think the thing the blackmailer is taking back is footage of us putting a bag of dirty clothes in a locker.

OWEN: Where would you even hide a camera? Because after there was that big thing with the PTA about only having security cameras at the front entrance of the school, you'd have to hide it pretty well.

ALLY: Why did the school decide that?

GEMMA: Privacy issues—lucky for us. If there were school security cameras anywhere inside, we'd be dead.

[*Silence.*]

OWEN: Let's move on.

MONDAY: 9:14 A.M.
TODD

> Mr. Smith will be coming to the closet for supplies in two minutes. Go to room 101 next door. Text when you are there.

Todd nearly threw open the door in his haste to get out, forgetting to check if anyone was outside. Mr. Smith, one of the janitors, did not like Todd, and Todd had no desire to run into him now. There had been several unfortunate incidents during Todd's time at Snow Valley Secondary, and even he could admit that Mr. Smith had the right to hold a grudge. Though all that mattered now was that it would be better for all of them if they weren't discovered in Mr. Smith's supply closet.

"Be more careful," Gemma hissed. But luckily the hallway was empty as they hurried to the classroom next to the closet.

Room 101 was Todd's homeroom, Mr. Patel's classroom, and it had a small graphic novel history library in the back, complete with two beanbag chairs. Once they were all inside, Owen closed the door and Todd let out a breath of relief that they'd made it. Then he headed straight for the back and flopped down on one of the beanbags. Gemma, whose phone seemed permanently in her hand, was already texting. A moment later all their phones vibrated.

Use the classroom phone to call the main office to report a package in locker A-18. Then text me.

"That's not good," Owen said, frowning. He was pacing again though it was less annoying in a bigger space.

"At least it's not illegal," Ally pointed out. She'd come over to stand by the bookcase. "And it's just a bag of clothes so maybe it's not that big a deal."

"Considering all the trouble the blackmailer has gone to getting in that locker, it probably is," Gemma pointed out, walking toward the phone. "But you're right, at least making the call isn't so bad."

She picked up the phone and pressed for the main office. Owen bumped into a desk and all three of them glared at him. He held up his hands and sat down in the chair, looking sheepish.

"Yes, I'd like to report a suspicious package in locker A-18," Gemma said crisply into the phone. Todd could hear Ms. Atkins, the school administrative assistant, speaking as Gemma hung up, then texted the blackmailer.

Owen popped back up and began wandering around the room touching things, which was annoying. "Do you guys have Mr. Patel for history?"

"Um, I'm in your class," Ally said.

Todd snorted and Gemma shook her head.

"Oh, yeah, that's right," Owen said, excited to be reminded instead of acting embarrassed—which was so typical Owen. "You made that poster on homing pigeons during the Revolutionary War."

Ally smiled. "Yeah, Mr. Patel is the best because I didn't want to do any of the topics he had listed so he said I could choose my own."

"Same—I did mine on the use of comics and art as propaganda," Owen said.

Todd had to admit this was kind of impressive. Owen was ridiculous but he was serious about comics and that was cool.

Ally nodded. "I remember. It was really good."

"You guys are lucky you have him," Gemma said. She was leaning against the wall by the phone. "I had him last year and he actually makes history stuff fun. This year I have Mr. Lane and he is supremely boring."

Todd heard the mop bucket being pushed down the hall and a moment later their phones vibrated.

Go back to the closet. Your first task is complete but don't relax just yet—the next one is coming to you at the end of snack. Be on the lookout for my instructions then.

It was 9:30, which meant they had fifteen minutes before the bell for morning snack.

"Great, so we just have to sit here and wait," Todd muttered once they were back in the small closet. Not that he wanted to follow more instructions from the maniac blackmailing them. But hanging around waiting for whatever came next just meant more time to worry. And Todd did not need that.

"Do you think we can go out for snack?" Gemma asked. "I have someone I really need to talk to."

Why she was acting like anything mattered more than following instructions to keep their secrets secret was beyond Todd—though chances were good her secret was no big deal compared with his.

"Yeah, I'm hungry," Owen said. He stood up and started pacing again around the small closet.

Todd rolled his eyes. There was no way he could eat anything until this was over. Obviously Owen's secret was something pretty minor-league as well. Todd was lucky Ally was as desperate as he was to keep the blackmailer quiet—otherwise he'd be in real trouble.

"We probably should, since we were all marked here at attendance today," Ally said. "Not that I could eat anything now. I hate waiting for bad things to happen—I'd so much rather just get it over with."

"Agree," Gemma said with a sigh.

Owen knocked over the mop bucket, making a loud clank.

"Shh!" Gemma practically shouted. "We don't want anyone coming in here."

"Stop moving around and sit down like a normal person," Todd snapped. He had the urge to shove Owen but kept it in check—Owen would probably yell and break something and get them caught.

"Sorry," Owen said, sitting back down next to Ally and at least having the sense to look like he meant it. "I'm what my dad calls a 'fidgeter.' My parents are the opposite, all chill—I kind of drive them bonkers sometimes."

"A lot of the time, I'd bet," Todd said with an edge.

But Owen just laughed. "Kind of, yeah—I'm probably adopted or something."

"What?" Ally asked in a voice that made Todd freeze. It was a voice that said, "Danger."

"Um, it was just a joke?" Owen asked more than stated. He glanced at Gemma but she too was looking at Ally carefully.

"That because you're different from your parents and annoying to them, you were adopted, like adopted kids are somehow lesser than biological kids? That's your joke?"

Todd could really see how Ally was good at working with animals—not only could she stay calm when things were stressful, she had a tone of voice that would make any living creature do exactly what she said, when she said it.

"I don't, I mean, I didn't," Owen fumbled, looking so dazed Todd felt a flicker of sympathy for him.

"Whatever, just don't do it again," Ally said, folding her arms over her chest. "I'm adopted and my parents didn't feel any differently about me than a kid with their DNA—same with my grandparents. I'm their family, end of story."

"Got it," Owen said, rubbing his face for a moment. "Actually that's how I feel about Jade—technically she's my stepsister but really she's just my sister."

This earned a smile from Ally, and Owen looked pleased. Todd hoped this meant Owen would stop talking but no luck there.

"So who do you guys think is behind this?" he asked.

At least he'd asked a good question. But judging from the silence, no one had an answer. Todd certainly didn't, and he'd been thinking about it ever since getting that stupid email.

"Maybe if we find out whose locker that was, we'd have a lead," Ally said finally. "But otherwise there haven't been any clues about who this person is."

"Or why they chose us and what their goal is," Gemma said. "I mean, why put a bag of dirty clothes in someone's locker?"

Again there were no answers.

Todd thought it might be nice if everyone was quiet for the last few minutes they were stuck in the closet, but of course Owen had other ideas.

"So who do you have to talk to at snack?" Owen asked Gemma.

"That's nothing you need to be concerned about," Gemma snapped. She'd been looking at her screen but now she jammed the phone into her pocket.

Todd had to admit he was also a bit curious who she was so invested in seeing and texting—did it have something to do with her secret? Not that he was dumb enough to ask.

"Well, can I be concerned that you quit basketball? You're really good," Owen went on.

"No, you can't be concerned about that," Gemma said, now even more annoyed. "I was tired of it, end of story."

"That doesn't make sense," Owen said, shaking his head.

Todd did not know why Owen didn't understand that sometimes you shut up instead of talking and making things worse. And why did he care so much what Gemma did in her free time? Todd himself could care less.

"It doesn't need to make sense to you, it's not your life," Gemma said, glaring at Owen. "And I think you have enough to worry about."

Todd snickered. "Yeah, like the clowns you hang out with."

Owen blinked. "My friends aren't clowns."

"They totally are," Todd said. He was angry just thinking about Owen's "friends" Matt, Caden, Paul, and especially James, who acted like they were better than everyone else. They were the ones who cut the cafeteria line themselves but then yelled at anyone else who did it. And last year Todd overheard James making a joke about the "losers who couldn't get real jobs" at Cassidy Trailer Park, where Todd and Mom lived. Obviously Todd had straightened out the situation, but he knew James still thought because he lived in the nice part of town and Todd did not, that he was better than Todd. Plus it was people like Owen's friends who made Mom's job harder, and nothing made Todd angrier than that.

"Caden's okay but James is mean," Gemma said, glancing quickly at her phone.

Todd nodded because while he had his doubts about Caden, James was truly bad news.

"He's a good guy," Owen said more firmly than he had said anything. Except when he was talking about drawing comics—he'd been pretty firm then too. "He's always had my back."

"Well, he's stabbed a lot of other people in the back," Gemma said. "He told everyone Lainie smelled bad after she wouldn't dance with him at the Halloween dance."

Todd really liked how Gemma said exactly what she thought. Especially when it meant serving Owen some much-needed truth. And then something occurred to him.

"Could James be the one blackmailing us?" he asked. "I could see him doing something like this."

"No, he—" Owen started, but Gemma spoke over him.

"James would never put together a plan this complicated," she said. "He's not that calculating—and if he wanted a bag of clothes in someone's locker, he'd put it there himself. But he really is a bully—I saw him try to kick a dog in the park, just because it was barking at his skateboard." She looked at Ally. "Can you report something like that? Because some people shouldn't be allowed near animals. Or be allowed to own them."

"I'm probably not the person to ask about that," Ally said, staring down at her hands, which were laced together in her lap.

That seemed like a weird response to Todd—wasn't she the perfect person to ask since she worked with rescued animals? Gemma seemed surprised as well. But then her phone vibrated and once again she was pulled into her screen, a big smile on her face as she read her text and then began to respond.

Owen inched closer to Ally and tried to peek past her to see who Gemma was texting. Tried and failed because Ally shoved him off.

"Sorry, I—"

"She's texting that guy she hangs out with so give her some space," Ally told him firmly. "And give me some space too."

"Gemma has a secret boyfriend?" Owen asked.

"No, I—" Gemma began, but it was too late. Ally was looking at Owen and had not seen Gemma's stricken expression.

"That guy in the high school—Miles, I think," Ally said. "He's a sophomore. They've been hanging out for a while."

And then several things happened at once: Gemma jumped to her feet, stuttering some kind of protest, and Owen's eyes widened, but for the first time he was speechless.

And Todd started to laugh.

OWEN

"There's nothing funny," Gemma hissed at Todd, who for some reason was going off like a hyena. Owen did not get Todd and didn't especially want to, though at this moment he was glad Todd was the one Gemma was mad at.

He was also glad the conversation about James had ended. Talking about James made him queasy.

Gemma spun around to take on Ally. Her hands were on her hips, her eyes were narrowed, and she was breathing in short bursts, none of which was a good sign.

Owen edged away from Ally, not wanting to accidentally get caught in Gemma's crossfire, then got up and went to stand by the mop bucket. The air was extra piney there but he didn't want to get close to Gemma or Todd, who had finally stopped laughing.

"What do you know about Miles and why did you just backstab me like that?" Gemma asked Ally in a shrill voice.

"I don't know anything about him," Ally said, her brows scrunching together. "I just saw you together a couple of times so I know you hang out with him. Did these guys not know or something?"

Ally was so genuinely bewildered by Gemma's response, Owen could now see why Todd was laughing.

"Ally, no one knew Gemma was sneaking around with some high school guy," Todd explained. "I bet that's her secret."

Ally paused, shook her head, and then the corners

of her mouth turned down. "Seriously? But I've seen you guys. How could I be the only one?"

"Because clearly you sneak around and spy on people," Gemma said sharply.

Owen was grateful Gemma's wrath was not headed in his direction—it had been bad enough when Ally was mad at him. And he hadn't even outed her secret. But he did have a question and he could not hold it in. "So wait, are you dating this older guy?"

"No, not that it's any of your business," Gemma hissed, "but we're just good friends."

"I guess I mostly did see you when I was on my way to the library during snack and lunch," Ally said, clearly thinking carefully about this. Unlike Owen, she did not seem fazed by Gemma's rage. Though this was probably because she was used to dealing with abused animals who got pretty snarly and aggressive when they first arrived at the sanctuary. "But I just assumed everyone knew. Don't you want people to know?"

If possible, Gemma radiated even more rage. "It's not for show! We're real friends. No one else understands or listens to him like I do. It's a very *mature* relationship." Even through the rage Owen could hear the pride in her voice at this last statement.

"Really?" Ally asked, seeming genuinely curious. Owen couldn't believe Ally was so not bothered by Gemma's fury—even he might have taken a minute before pressing on with the conversation. Clearly Ally was braver than he was.

"Yes, really," Gemma hissed.

"Okay, well I'm sure you know what you're doing," Ally said. Owen relaxed the littlest bit because now maybe they'd stop fighting. "But when the guy is that much older there's a risk for a power imbalance, so be careful."

Well, Ally did not pull punches. And she was not afraid to say what she thought.

"She's right," Todd said to Gemma. He was frowning slightly.

"Like you two know anything about mature relationships," Gemma said dismissively.

Todd shrugged. "He sounds pretty immature to me if he doesn't have any friends his own age," he said.

"No one cares what you think," Gemma said witheringly.

It would be a good idea to stay quiet right now, and Owen knew this. But something finally made sense and he had to say it. "That's why you quit basketball.

So you could be in drama club and do the play—you want to be with Miles more."

Now Gemma's razor-sharp gaze was directed at him. "Just drop the basketball already, Owen."

Owen cowered, glad he hadn't mentioned that he and his team friends had set up their yearly betting pool on whether the girls or boys team would win more games. Owen had gone with the girls because of Gemma, so this Miles guy had really messed up his odds—but Ally spoke right up.

"Seriously?" she asked, sounding annoyed. "You gave up something you love to hang out with a guy?"

Owen had to admit Ally had a point here.

Gemma folded her arms over her chest. "This conversation is closed and you are all sworn to secrecy about my relationship."

Owen had more to say but this time he managed to keep his mouth shut. The whole thing seemed like a bum deal for Gemma. Maybe this guy was nice but then why was he okay with her giving up basketball?

"Why don't we talk about your secret, Todd, or whatever it is *you're* so eager to keep quiet, Ally?" Gemma asked in a spiteful voice, glaring at each of them in turn. "And what about you, Owen? Want to tell us why you're here, what you have to lose?"

Owen opened his mouth but the bell for snack rang before he could decline Gemma's offer.

"I'm out of here," Gemma muttered, pushing past Todd and wrenching open the closet.

"Find us in the cafeteria before snack ends," Ally called. "We need to be ready for our text."

But Gemma did not reply.

GEMMA

Gemma's heart was pounding like she'd just done a warm-up drill and her face was hot as she stalked down the hall. She heard Ally but didn't bother responding. She had nothing to say to any of those people, *nothing*. And the fact that she still had to help them complete whatever stupid instructions were coming next made her rigid with fury. To think she'd actually started to like Ally! Power imbalance—what did that even mean? Miles cared about her. It wasn't about power, it was about how intuitive she was—that's what Miles said when she listened and encouraged him. It was *adult*, something Ally was obviously too immature to understand.

Gemma had met Miles at the town pool over the summer. She'd noticed him immediately, with his shaggy brown hair, big blue eyes, and easy smile. He worked at the snack bar, and after Gemma had nearly spent all her birthday money on bruised bananas and bags of stale chips, day after day, he'd finally started talking to her. At first it was casual, with Gemma asking questions about high school and working at the pool. But soon Miles was seeking her out on his breaks to complain about his stingy boss or the way his mom tried to control him all the time. Gemma was thrilled he'd chosen her to confide in. And she'd made sure to exchange numbers at the end of the summer. The first week of school when he'd texted to report that his schedule was unfair, she'd suggested they meet up to talk about it more at school. Now Gemma made it clear that she'd always be waiting for him at their place under the far stairwell at the start of both break and lunch. And nothing was more wonderful than the days he could be there too.

Gemma turned the corner into the central hallway, which was now crowded with students heading to the cafeteria for snack. "Hey, Gem," Amirah called, touching Gemma's shoulder as she passed with Mei, Bianca, and Steph, her teammates on basketball and Gemma's closest friends. "We miss you on the court."

"Miss you guys too," Gemma said. She didn't appreciate the reminder of basketball after all the idiotic things Owen had said about her quitting, but she did miss seeing more of Amirah and the others. And playing. But Gemma could play basketball anytime and the chance to be with Miles every afternoon at drama—well, it was much more important. Not that they could sit together or talk if anyone was around, obviously. Miles would never allow rumors to hurt Gemma. But it would be so easy to sneak off for a few minutes, just the two of them, to talk and that—that was certainly worth missing a few stupid basketball games.

Owen was just too immature to get that.

The thing was, no one got it. Or they wouldn't if they knew. Miles said their friendship was special and it would be ruined if other people knew—they'd get all worked up about the age difference between Miles and Gemma. And if her parents ever found out? There were not enough fiery words to describe the explosion that would take place. Yes, it was just a friendship, but Gemma knew Miles cared about her deeply and one day, when she was older, he probably, maybe, hopefully, would be her boyfriend. Mom, who could read Gemma like she read her favorite magazines, would see Gemma's true feelings in a second, and Gemma and Miles would be torn apart. And Gemma would do anything to prevent that. Which was why she was going along with the blackmailer and why, even though it made her grit her teeth, she'd meet up with Todd, Owen, and that backstabber Ally before snack ended.

Gemma pushed through the crowd, heading away from the cafeteria toward her meeting spot with Miles, under the staircase near the library. Where stupid Ally had seen them. Gemma was actually surprised about this—she and Miles had been pretty careful about not being seen. There were some extremely nosy and obnoxious people in seventh grade who would make a huge deal of it if they saw—Alyssa, for example, who was the biggest gossip ever. Or Vivi, goody-goody of the century who was always sniffing around trying to get people in trouble so teachers would like her more. Vivi was pretty much Gemma's least favorite person at

Snow Valley Secondary after last year's incident where she got Gemma called out for a dress code violation. Everyone knew the dress code was stupid and sexist but when Vivi made a big deal about Gemma's tank top straps being too thin, Ms. Blake had had no choice but to send Gemma to the office. Vivi was the kind of person to sneak around spying on people and then tell the world, not Ally. Well, in fairness maybe Ally hadn't been sneaking and maybe she hadn't exactly told the world—but still, Gemma would have expected better from her.

The question now was whether Gemma should tell Miles a few students had just learned about their friendship. Of course people who were mature like Gemma and Miles should be honest about everything. But Miles got anxious about anyone finding out about them. The few precious minutes they would hopefully have together, if Miles was able to get away and meet her at all, would be eaten up by his worries. Which didn't seem fair to him really—Gemma was confident Ally wouldn't tell her secret. After all, who would she tell? And Todd and Owen would keep their mouths closed—plus who would believe them over Gemma anyway? They were both so immature. No, it was best for Gemma to protect Miles from something so insignificant. Especially when what she needed right now was to be reassured that her relationship wasn't a power imbalance like those fools in the closet had claimed. Gemma knew they were wrong, of course she did. Being with Miles, hearing about his morning, what was on his mind, how none of his friends had ever understood him the way Gemma did, well, who wouldn't want that?

But Miles never showed up.

ALLY

"I get that sometimes his pranks are over the top but he's not a bad guy," Owen was saying. The cafeteria was extra loud after the quiet of spending most of the morning in the closet, and Ally's temples were throbbing. She rested her head in her hands, eyes closed, wishing she was anywhere but here and with anyone but the two boys arguing across the table from her.

"He is and you're no better if you hang out with him," Todd said. Like Ally, he was not eating.

Owen, meanwhile, was switching between orange juice, Doritos, and a packet of M&Ms. Just thinking about that combination of tastes made Ally want to swear off eating for good. He'd gotten the snacks when he'd made a quick detour to say hi to his friends, which had kicked off the boys' latest disagreement.

"If you're talking about James, you're right."

Ally opened her eyes and saw that Gemma had arrived and was settling onto the seat next to Ally. She had a packet of sunflower seeds that she ripped open with a surprising amount of force, spraying seeds across the table. And if anything, she looked even more annoyed to be there than Ally.

"Back off, he's my friend," Owen said irritably. "And at least he doesn't hang out with underage girls." He stuffed a handful of Doritos into his mouth, then choked on them, spraying orange crumbs across the table.

Gemma leaned over, closer to Owen. "First off, that's gross. Second of all, shut up. Third of all, Miles is not an adult so that makes no sense, and fourth of all, *shut up*."

Ally wanted to say something to calm things down and to support Gemma, particularly since she felt pretty bad about having spilled Gemma's secret. Though really, Gemma and Miles hadn't done a great job keeping their friendship secret. Ally had no idea how the blackmailer had discovered her own secret, but Gemma's would not have been hard to uncover. But anyway, while Ally wanted to support Gemma, it wasn't possible because she agreed 100 percent with the boys: Hanging out with someone a year or two younger when you were both in high school was one thing but a sophomore having a secret friendship with a seventh grader? It was just complete yuck.

Owen might have had more to say but he was still hacking on the Doritos and trying to wipe off the table.

"Owen's right," Todd said, looking evenly at Gemma.

"What do you know about it?" Gemma spat out the words.

"My dad was a total deadbeat who left my mom for a twenty-year-old because he couldn't handle a relationship with someone who was his equal," Todd said coolly, spreading his hands out over the table. "He wanted someone to talk to who wouldn't talk back and tell him when he was being an idiot, which was a lot. He wanted hero worship, not a real relationship. *That's* what I know about it."

Ally was so surprised at this revelation she had trouble not letting her mouth fall open in shock, like someone in a cartoon. Because that was the first personal thing Todd had shared. Well, besides wanting a cat, but that wasn't exactly a big deal. This information about his dad though? That was a big deal.

Understandably Gemma was not sure how to respond and was pressing her lips together. And then, not surprisingly, Owen, who had recovered from the Doritos incident, spoke up.

"Wow, that must have completely sucked," he said in a typical Owen way.

Ally looked at her hands, waiting for Todd to yell at Owen like he always did when Owen spoke up, but to her surprise Todd laughed. "Yeah, that pretty much sums it up," he said.

"My dad left too," Owen told him. "But his new girlfriend is his age. At least she looks his age. I never actually asked. She's a school principal in Albany where they live though, so I'm hoping they break up soon."

They all laughed at that and for the first time Ally realized there was something sweet about Owen, how he said whatever popped into his head without worrying about looking dumb. He kind of reminded her of some of the younger dogs at the sanctuary, not that he was stupid, more that he was open and good-natured. Which made it strange that he hung out with a jerk like James. Because that one Gemma *had* called right. Just last week James had pushed past Ally in the hall, causing her to stumble, and instead of apologizing had told her to "dress like a girl."

"Hey, Leo," Owen called as Leo walked past their table to toss out his snack wrappers. Leo, who was nice to everyone, glanced at Owen, then at Todd, Ally, and Gemma, and instead of answering, hurried past.

"That was weird," Gemma said, peering after him.

"Yeah," Owen said, sounding puzzled. "He lives down the block so sometimes we walk to school together and he's usually pretty friendly."

"Maybe he doesn't like guys who have annoying friends," Todd said.

"Or maybe you punched him once and he remembers it," Owen shot back.

Todd frowned slightly, looking after Leo. "I don't think so," he said.

The fact that he wasn't sure was slightly disturbing.

It seemed to Ally that you should remember everyone you'd ever assaulted.

The bell rang and Ally's stomach lurched. The text would be arriving any second. And sure enough, as the crush of students surged toward the cafeteria exit, her phone vibrated. It was the perfect time to check, with all the chaos and only a few cafeteria aides now just eager for the place to clear out. So Ally, Gemma, Todd, and Owen each pulled out their phones and carefully read the message.

> Split up. Gemma and Ally, grab two anti-bullying posters—not any other kind—and go to the girls' bathroom back by the auditorium. Todd and Owen, go to room 104. Text the minute you get there. And move: You have five minutes.

Ally's hands were shaking as she stuffed her phone into her back pocket. The auditorium was at the far end of the school and with the crowds in the hall they were going to have to hustle to make it. Meanwhile room 104 was right around the corner, next to the main office.

"Hurry," Gemma said, pushing her way through the crowd. Ally followed.

Tabby, a popular girl, called, "Hey, Gem," as they passed, and gave them a funny look. Ally wasn't dumb—she knew Tabby was surprised to see Gemma with a social nobody like Ally, but on Explorer's Day people could be together for all kinds of reasons. Yet another thing that made the blackmailer's choice of this day such a good one.

A group of eighth-grade boys ran past and one of them knocked a poster down. Ally reached down to grab it, thinking their mission had just gotten easier, but unfortunately it was for a Thanksgiving food drive. They were going to have to pull down the anti-bullying posters, yet another school rule they were going to break.

"Keep watch and I'll grab this one," Gemma said in a low voice, coming to a stop in front of an anti-bullying poster.

"Okay," Ally said, doing a quick scan of the hallway. It was clearing as students reached their classrooms for the second part of Explorer's Day immersion classes. No one appeared to be looking at them and no teachers were in sight. But then Ally caught sight of Vivi. "Wait one second," she told Gemma.

Last week Vivi and Ally had been assigned a social studies worksheet to complete in class, and Vivi had accused Ally of not doing her half of the work. Ally had been particularly tired—a new bunny had arrived at the sanctuary the night before and she'd been up late with her grandparents helping settle the little rabbit. Ally had apologized but Vivi was not forgiving. And ever since she had made a point of glaring at Ally when she passed. If she saw Ally doing something fishy with posters, she'd definitely want to know more.

But Vivi did not notice Ally, probably because she was scolding a sixth grader for running in the hall. A moment later she walked into her classroom and Ally let out a sigh of relief. "Go ahead," she said to Gemma.

Gemma pulled the poster down in one fast movement, then passed it to Ally. A second one was about three feet away and Gemma headed for it. Ally realized there were so many anti-bullying posters on the walls it was possible no one would notice these two were gone. She hoped not anyway.

"Come on," Gemma said, nearly running to the girls' bathroom at the end of the hall. Ally was on her heels and a moment later they were pushing open the heavy wooden door.

"Text," Gemma ordered. She already had her phone out.

Ally scrambled for hers and typed *Here* as fast as she could.

And then she held her breath, waiting for the reply.

CHAPTER 5

MONDAY: 1:03 P.M.

RECORDING PART 4

OWEN: [*Laughing.*] I can't believe you guys had to make the toilet overflow by stuffing posters in it—I wish I'd been there to see that. [*Muffled sound.*] Hey, didn't we agree no punching?

GEMMA: That was never agreed upon, no.

ALLY: It was really gross. We got out of there fast. And the last thing we had to do was make a call to Ms. Montenegro so she'd leave the office. She sounded really annoyed about that.

OWEN: Probably because you interrupted her plotting the downfall of Principal Grace.

ALLY: Right, she said on the phone that she wants him to leave. I wonder—

TODD: Guys, focus! The only question right now is why you had to clog the toilets with anti-bullying posters and not just any kind of poster. Does anyone have any ideas?

OWEN: Maybe people got sick of hearing about not bullying all the time. Principal Grace talks about it endlessly and it's getting old.

GEMMA: Yeah, but remember what happened with Cody and bullying—Principal Grace must've gotten in big trouble for that.

OWEN: Yeah, you can't get a second Gold Star Award if your school has bullying.

GEMMA: But getting back on topic: Let's move on to what we did next.

[*Slight groan from Ally.*]

GEMMA: I know, I don't want to think about it either. Because the other things were questionable, but what we did in the office? That was *definitely illegal.*

MONDAY: 10:24 A.M.
OWEN

Owen and Todd headed down the hall toward room 104. It seemed like everyone else was moving the other way, reminding Owen of the time his family had gone to the beach at Cape Cod and he'd had to fight against the waves getting back to shore. A group of girls were laughing and one of them bumped into Todd.

"Watch it," he said sharply.

The girl was about to respond when she appeared to realize who she was talking to. Instead she ducked her head and hurried after her friends, several of whom glared at Todd from a safe distance.

Todd really did have a reputation.

Sophia, one of Owen's least favorite people in the grade, was frowning at Todd. "You could be nicer to the younger kids," she told Todd primly. Sophia, along with her best friend, Vivi, who stood next to her, were two of the only people not intimidated by Todd. Or anyone, probably because they had a reign of terror reporting every little thing their classmates tried to get away with. Vivi had gotten Owen's phone confiscated in class more than once and had been quick to notify Mr. Wagner when Owen was whispering with Caden instead of watching the boring class video last week. Weirdly she did not add anything to what Sophia was saying to Todd now, but looked away, shifting her weight like she was nervous about something.

"If I was interested in what you thought, I'd ask," Todd informed Sophia coldly.

"You are—" Sophia began, her eyes narrowing.

But Vivi tugged her arm. "Come on, let's just go," she said. "What goes around comes around." She smirked slightly as she pulled her friend down the hall.

"People really like you," Owen told Todd, who scrunched his mouth up like he'd eaten a rotten peanut.

"Like I care what they think," he said. He was right—it wasn't like anyone liked Vivi and Sophia, and they hated pretty much everyone. Though that whole "what goes around comes around" thing seemed weird. If Vivi thought someone had something coming, she usually just told a teacher.

They'd reached room 104 and Owen pulled out his phone to text. He anxiously waited for the response. He did not want to be asked to do anything like break into a locker again. A moment later the phone vibrated:

> Call the main office. Tell Ms. Atkins that a parent is at the far exit by the gym, very upset about an earlier incident. Then hang up and go back to the janitor's closet.

He released his breath—this was no big deal. In fact, Owen was famous (well, famous at home) for his imitation of both his dad and his stepdad.

"I've got it," he told Todd.

Todd shrugged and wandered to the row of windows that looked out over the football field while Owen picked up the classroom phone and pressed for the main office. As it rang he had a momentary panic attack because what if Dana answered? She knew him from back when he hung out with her brother and might recognize his voice. But then he remembered high schoolers only did morning volunteer hours, so he was ready when Ms. Atkins picked up.

"Yes," Owen began in a deep voice, "I need to report a parent at the exit by the gym. He's very upset, yelling about an earlier incident and threatening legal action." That last part hadn't been in the instructions but Owen thought it sounded good.

"What?" Ms. Atkins shrieked. Owen jumped and hurriedly hung up the phone. Maybe it hadn't been so good after all.

"Smooth," Todd said, snickering. Apparently he'd heard Ms. Atkins from across the room, which was kind of embarrassing.

"We should get back to the closet," Owen said, straightening his t-shirt, just to do something with his hands.

Todd nodded and they headed out.

Owen had assumed the girls would be there but when they arrived at the small, dark room, it was empty. And very quiet. Which was a little uncomfortable.

Owen pulled out his phone to cover up the awkward moment, but when he looked up a minute later, he saw that Todd hadn't taken out his phone. Which made Owen feel even more awkward. What was wrong with Todd that he wasn't taking his phone out? Was it rude for Owen to keep using his? Was he supposed to actually *talk* to Todd, just the two of them?

"So, ah, this whole thing is really weird, right?" Owen asked, shoving his phone back in his pocket.

Todd looked disgusted by the idiocy of Owen's statement but at least he nodded. Owen was trying to figure out what to say next, when Todd spoke.

"*Watchmen*," he said.

"Um, what watch men?" Owen asked, looking around. Were they being watched?

Todd laughed. "*Watchmen*, the graphic novel. I've been trying to figure out my favorite since you said you're into them and I'm going with *Watchmen*."

Owen had never properly understood the word *flabbergasted* until this moment. Because not only was Todd starting a conversation with him, an interesting one no less, Todd liked *Watchmen*! Which was, of course, one of Owen's favorites (any real fan of the genre worshipped *Watchmen*) but also the last thing he would have expected from Todd. Because *Watchmen*— well, it was kind of deep actually. None of his friends had read it. *No one* he knew had read it.

"It's amazing—the thing with the squid?" Owen said eagerly, taking a step toward Todd and nearly kicking over the mop bucket again. But this time Todd didn't even notice.

"Right?" he said, pressing his hands together, more enthusiastic than Owen had ever seen him.

"I did not see that coming. Why do you think Dr. Manhattan—"

But he was interrupted by the door opening and the girls coming in, both breathless from running.

"We're talking about this later," Owen told Todd, who nodded. Then he turned to Gemma and Ally. "So what did you guys have to do?"

"Clog the toilet with anti-bullying posters," Ally said, her lips curling as her nose wrinkled at the memory.

Both Todd and Owen burst out laughing.

"Super not funny," Gemma snapped. She had been inspecting her shoes, probably for toilet water, but paused to glare at them both.

"What did you guys have to do?" Ally asked, leaning against the wall by the sink, which Owen was starting to think of as her spot. They'd really spent a lot of time in this closet today.

"Call Ms. Atkins and tell her a parent was upset by the back exit," Owen said.

Ally rolled her eyes and sagged back against the wall. "Yet another reason to hate this blackmailer—he gave me and Gemma the worst job."

"He or she," Gemma pointed out. "Though it does

seem like only a guy could be this annoying," she added, giving Todd and Owen a sour look.

That was when their phones all vibrated.

Owen pulled his out of his pocket so fast it nearly slipped out of his hands.

Five minutes ago I hid three things in Ms. Piedmont's room. Todd, you keep watch at the door. Gemma, you get the flash drive under the fake potted plant on her desk. Owen, you find the yellow post-it stuck to the back of the smart board. Memorize what it says, then shred the post-it into the recycling bin. Ally, in the garbage there is a sealed plastic bag with a pair of latex gloves. Get the gloves and throw out the bag. Text when you have everything and hurry—you only have five minutes.

Todd leaned toward the door to listen for anyone in the hall outside, then pulled it open. "Let's go," he said, waving them out impatiently. All traces of his friendliness with Owen were gone.

Todd led the way to room 125, which was across the hall from the main office. Owen anxiously glanced in but then remembered their calls—no one would be in the office now.

Todd opened the door and waved everyone through, then stood just inside, keeping his eyes on the hallway. "Hurry," he said again. "We're at four minutes and three seconds."

Gemma raced to the desk while Ally grabbed the bag from the metal pail next to Ms. Piedmont's desk. Ms. Piedmont taught sixth-grade world history, a class Owen hadn't minded, and her room was decorated with posters, small artifacts, and art from around the world. It was normally a place Owen found relaxing and pleasant but now it was making him nauseous. He was not good at memorizing things—what if he couldn't get the Post-it message into his brain in time? Would the blackmailer somehow know if he kept it instead of shredding it?

After running a shaking hand behind the smart board, he felt the small paper and pulled it off. Then he read, "GoldStarPrincipal1." Which made no sense but at least was easy to remember, so that was a relief.

But that feeling was short-lived.

"We have less than a minute!" Todd barked.

"I've got it," Owen said, tapping his temple to show

the message was secure. Then he shredded the Post-it. Ally held up the gloves but Gemma looked like she was about to pass out.

"I can't find the drive," she whispered, her face an alarming shade of gray.

"Come on," Todd snapped, rushing over and sweeping a hand across the desk.

"Did it get knocked off?" Ally asked, kneeling down to look.

"Does anyone have it?" Owen asked a moment later, acid crawling at the back of his throat.

"No," Ally wailed.

Todd grabbed the plant and Owen cowered, because it looked like Todd was about to hurl it across the room. But then something fell from the bottom of the planter onto the desk with a small clink.

"Got it," Todd said breathlessly, grabbing the drive.

Owen had out his phone and was texting the blackmailer before Todd had finished speaking. Then he leaned against the desk to slow his heart and calm his stomach. Hopefully the next task wouldn't be as heart attack–inducing. But when the text came, it was clear that things were going from bad to worse. Because their next instructions were chilling:

> Go to Principal Grace's office. Text me when you are all inside.

GEMMA

Gemma was alarmingly close to fainting as they hurried down the hall and into the empty main office. Not finding the flash drive right away had been more terrifying than the time her little sister, Kate, had hidden under Gemma's bed, dressed in her Halloween zombie costume, and rolled out moaning and clawing wildly after Gemma had turned out the light.

And this next task wasn't doing anything to help her recover.

"We're really not allowed back there," Ally said in a shaky voice as Todd rushed around the long wooden desk that served as a barrier between the area where students were permitted and the area where they were not. As he cleared the corner he nearly knocked down the mini trophy the school had won for the Gold Star Award (for some stupid reason the award had both a mini and the majorly huge trophy).

"Careful," Owen said. He was right behind Todd and managed to keep the trophy from falling.

Ally was next and she looked back at Gemma.

"I don't want to either but we don't have a choice," Gemma told her, because even though she'd only known her a few short hours, she could tell what Ally was thinking.

Ally nodded and ran after Todd and Owen, Gemma right behind her. They passed Ms. Atkins's desk, covered with files and an ugly pair of cacti, and the open door of Ms. Montenegro's office, which was empty.

And then they were all inside Principal Grace's office, a place Gemma had been in only once, when she was co-running a bake sale to raise money for basketball uniforms. It looked a lot more ominous today, the Gold Star Award poster somehow sinister in its bright sheen.

Owen had already texted the blackmailer and a moment later their phones vibrated.

Todd, put on the gloves. Then open Principal Grace's computer with the password Owen memorized. Text when you are in.

"Please tell me we are not hacking into the principal's computer," Ally said in a slightly shrill voice.

"I think that's why Todd has to wear the gloves,"

Owen said, "so no one can trace fingerprints." He seemed to think this would comfort Ally but she looked as wobbly as Gemma felt.

"What's the password?" Todd asked in a grim voice.

"GoldStarPrincipal1," Owen recited.

Gemma was momentarily distracted by how weird that was. "That's really his password?" she asked as Todd sat down in the desk chair.

"Someone has a pretty big ego," Owen said, shaking his head.

Todd had snapped on the gloves and was reaching out but Ally put her hands over the keyboard. "Guys, no, we can't do this. The rules we already broke were bad enough but this is actually illegal."

"It doesn't matter," Todd said mechanically. "We have to follow instructions."

"No, we don't, not when it's this serious," Ally snapped. Her hands were trembling but still blocking Todd from accessing the computer. "We could go to prison!"

Ally sounded fierce and normally Gemma would not mess with that. But in this case Todd was right— they had to follow instructions.

"Move!" Todd said loudly, slapping his palm down on the desk. "We're running out of time!"

This was going from bad to worse.

"Ally, Todd's right," Owen said, his gaze shifting between Ally and Todd. "We all hate this but we won't get caught if we just do what we're told."

Ally bit her lip, which Gemma decided meant she was wavering, so Gemma added on.

"Ally, the blackmailer planned this out really carefully—it's not in her or his interest to get us busted for hacking," Gemma added. "They need us to succeed, so if we just do what they say, it'll be okay."

"It's still wrong," Ally said, but she sounded less certain.

"Not as wrong as what the blackmailer is doing," Owen said.

"Or what will happen if we don't do it and the blackmailer tells our secrets," Gemma said.

Ally slowly pulled back her hands and Todd practically dove onto the keyboard. Gemma smiled at Owen: Crisis averted.

Todd was already at the keyboard typing. "We're in," he said.

Gemma hastily texted the blackmailer and a moment later their next instructions arrived.

Put in the flash drive and download the file "PP" into the Explorer's Day folder on the desktop. Then eject the drive, destroy it, and go back to the closet.

Todd was already shoving the drive into the keyboard. He waited, then clicked on "PP," which was the only folder on the drive. They waited, silently, as the file downloaded.

Gemma's insides felt like an eel was slithering around her organs, leaving a trail of slime in its wake. She looked away from the computer, at the chair in front of the desk where kids had to sit if they were in trouble. Normal trouble, not illegal trouble. The four of them would not be in this office if they were caught—they'd be down at the police station. The eel was now biting at Gemma's insides and she pressed her hands against her stomach to keep from puking.

The file was finally downloaded and Todd quickly ejected the drive and stuffed it, then the gloves, into his pocket. "Done," he said, and for the first time

Gemma heard a tremor in his voice. What he'd had to do for them had clearly not been easy on him.

"Thanks, Todd," Gemma said.

Todd looked at her, his brows raised, but before he could speak, they all heard it: footsteps coming down the hall, straight for the main office.

TODD

"Hide," Owen hissed, blinking rapidly as he looked around wildly.

"Don't be an idiot," Gemma hissed back, but she was also looking around frantically, like maybe a secret exit would suddenly appear.

Ally, meanwhile, had frozen in place, right in front of Ms. Montenegro's office, and looked like she was about to have a heart attack.

"Guys, get to the other side of the desk," Todd directed. His heart was thumping—it still hadn't quieted from breaking into Principal Grace's computer—and the thought of getting caught behind the barrier that separated the students-allowed area from the no-students-allowed area made Todd worry

Ally might not be the only one having a heart attack today.

He was first to race around the wooden barrier, Gemma on his heels and Owen behind her. It took Ally a moment to unfreeze and Todd was worried she wasn't going to make it—the footsteps were right outside, so close they could hear voices. And one of those voices belonged to Principal Grace.

But Ally was fast—maybe you had to be working with animals, because she was lightning once she got going. So when Principal Grace and Ms. Atkins walked in, all four of them were on the right side of the barrier. Breathing hard, but still, the right side.

Todd was smiling with relief at this but then he saw the look on Ms. Atkins's face and heard the sharp breath Principal Grace drew in. Which was when Todd realized that while being on the right side was better than being on the wrong side, being in the office at all was going to take some explaining.

"What exactly are the four of you doing here when you should be in your Explorer's classrooms?" Principal Grace asked. His words were to all of them but he was looking straight at Todd. Unfortunately this was far from his first time in this office and most of his meetings with the principal had not exactly gone well. Plus the principal had a certain smell, a weird mix of cinnamon, pepper, and leather from some kind of soap or shampoo, that always made Todd cough. So while Todd wanted to look responsible and innocent, instead his eyes began to water and his face scrunched up as he was attacked by a choking fit.

Gemma whacked him on the back, apparently trying to help, but she just made Todd hack away even harder.

"We were just, ah," she began. "Well, we were looking for," she stammered. Todd could tell she had no idea where to go with this and he realized this could be a disaster. Not that he could do anything about it when he was heaving up a lung.

"We were looking for Ms. Montenegro," Owen said. His voice was tinny and high but at least he had said something that made sense. Kind of. Because they had no reason to find Ms. Montenegro but at least she wasn't here to discover that.

"Is there something we can help you with?" Ms. Atkins asked. Out of his watering eyes Todd could see that she was stepping away from him. Everyone had gotten a Covid vaccine by now, but coughing still made most people anxious.

"No, thanks," Owen said a little too quickly. "We'll just, ah, take Todd to the water fountain and then get back to class."

"Make it snappy," Principal Grace said. "You want to make sure to pull your weight getting your presentation ready for the assembly and not put all that work onto others." Again he was looking at Todd, who nodded even though he felt like coughing in the principal's face.

"What is wrong with you?" Gemma asked Todd once they were safely in the hall.

"I think he's just allergic to Principal Grace," Owen said. The color was starting to come back to his face.

Todd was finally able to stop coughing now that they were away from that smell, but a snort of laughter made him start up again. He'd always thought Owen was useless—in fairness Todd thought most people at Snow Valley Secondary were useless—but it turned out Owen was not so bad.

"Hurry before some other teacher comes to ask why we're not in class," Ally said through gritted teeth as she hustled down the hall. Todd followed, cracking the drive in half and then stopping to crush each piece under his heel. He scooped up the bits and tossed them in two separate trash cans. Which had to count as fully destroying the drive.

Once they were safely back in the closet, Ally on the floor by the sink, Gemma next to her, Owen by that stupid mop bucket, and Todd closest to the door, they looked at each other.

"What," Gemma asked, her hands clenched up in front of her, "did we just do?"

CHAPTER 6

MONDAY: 1:08 P.M.

RECORDING PART 5

ALLY: So how illegal is it to hack into someone's computer and download a file you got from a sinister blackmailer?

GEMMA: Super illegal.

OWEN: I could check on my phone.

GEMMA: Or we could just make sure no one ever figures out it was us.

ALLY: That would be easier if we knew who was behind this.

GEMMA: Todd, do you have any idea what was in that file we downloaded? That might tell us something.

TODD: No, I was going too fast to open it or anything.

GEMMA: What would someone want us to load onto the principal's computer?

OWEN: Maybe he's secretly a serial killer and it's a list of his trophies.

ALLY: His *what*? Are there serial killer awards?

OWEN: No, it's this thing they do of collecting talismans from their victims.

GEMMA: That is both gross and irrelevant.

OWEN: She asked.

GEMMA: It was irrelevant when you first brought it up. Principal Grace is not a serial killer.

OWEN: But do we know this for sure?

GEMMA: Yes! He's way too obsessed with his Gold Star Award to have time to stalk and murder people.

TODD: That *would* be pretty time-consuming.

GEMMA: Guys, focus. What could be in that file that was so crucial someone blackmailed us to hack Principal Grace's computer?

[*Silence.*]

ALLY: You know what I'm wondering—how did the blackmailer know all this, not just how to hack but Principal Grace's password and what folders he has on his desktop? Seriously, who *is* this person?

MONDAY: 10:58 A.M.
ALLY

They had been back in the closet for less than a minute when their phones vibrated.

> Good job. One last task to go: Be in the front row at this afternoon's Explorer's Day presentation. Someone's going to steal the spotlight.

"What does *that* mean?" Todd muttered, stuffing

his phone back in his pocket and then rubbing his forehead. Ally figured he probably had a headache from all the crimes they'd committed so far today. She certainly did.

"It's a theater term for hogging the attention," Gemma said.

"I know the definition of 'steal the spotlight,'" Todd snapped. "I'm asking what the blackmailer means when they say it—I doubt they're going to be up on stage telling everyone what they did today, and obviously we're not going up there."

"I don't know what they mean but it's not good," Ally said. She was slightly damp and realized that her anxiety at hacking into the principal's office had resulted in sweat slithering down her back and sides. Gross. Hopefully she didn't smell gross too. She was too close to Gemma, who smelled like tropical fruit, to check.

"As long as it keeps our secrets safe, I guess we just sit there and see," Gemma said with a sigh. "At least we don't have to do anything else illegal."

That was a good point.

"Do you think we should go to lunch and Showcases?" Owen asked.

After lunch each Explorer's class met for thirty-five minutes to finalize their work and then a few volunteers went to set up displays in the gym. When they were complete the whole school would go to check out the Showcases for twenty minutes before heading to the auditorium for the big presentation slideshow.

"Yeah, that way it looks like we were just in our groups all day," Gemma said. "So we're not just suddenly showing up for the presentation slideshow."

"I think Gemma's right," Ally agreed. She wasn't sure of course. But it seemed like if they held up their end of the bargain, the blackmailer had to back off.

"Okay, but remember Gemma also believes this guy Miles is actually her friend," Todd pointed out.

Ally sucked in her breath because Gemma was not going to be okay with that.

Sure enough, Gemma flew to her feet and stalked over to Todd. "You're all about my secret but how about you tell us yours, so we can all judge you and tell *you* what a loser you are," she spat out.

"Guys," Owen said nervously, looking back and forth between them. "Stop."

But Todd was already holding up his hands, clearly not interested in getting into a big fight. "Whatever, I just think that guy isn't a real friend, but it's your life."

That was not enough for Gemma, who put her hands on her hips. "Yes, it's my life and my business and I'll thank you to stay out of it. But since you know so much, I'm serious, tell us your secret."

Todd shook his head. "No," he said. "Your secret is a joke compared with mine."

"Really?" Gemma asked icily. "A joke?"

"Yeah, so what if you have a stupid crush on a high school guy? My secret wouldn't just blow up my life, it would blow up my mom's and everything she works for and thinks is—" Todd stopped abruptly and shook his head. "The point is, my secret isn't just about me."

Ally drew in a slow breath because clearly the stakes were high for Todd. His secret would have actual fall-out for someone he loved.

Just like Ally's.

"I think that's probably a bit of an exaggeration," Gemma said, rolling her eyes. "I mean, your mom's an adult and unless there's something wrong with her—"

"There is *nothing* wrong with my mom," Todd said,

his voice so ferocious Ally found herself pulling her knees a little tighter in her seat on the floor.

"I didn't mean—" Gemma began.

"Drop it," Todd said in the ferocious voice.

Gemma's hands slid slowly off her hips, and while she didn't look happy, she didn't keep asking Todd questions.

Though that might have been because Owen started talking, babbling really, in a way that Ally realized was sheer nerves—clearly Owen did not like it when people argued.

"Wait, Todd, does your mom work at Canon Market? Lydia Hanley?" he asked. "I think I've seen her there, at the register. She always wears a rabbit pin on her uniform and she laughs a lot."

Todd was very still. "Yeah, that's her," he said.

And while this voice was not ferocious, it also had an obvious tone that said, very clearly, "Back off." If Todd's mom was a cashier at the local grocery, he'd probably gotten teased about it more than once. And it couldn't be an easy job—during Covid it had been actually dangerous, but now, when it was safe again, cashiers weren't always treated very well. Ally's grandparents were always kind to workers at stores and restaurants or wherever. But not everyone in Snow Valley was the same.

Not surprisingly, though, Owen didn't pick up on Todd's "drop it now" vibe.

"That is so cool!" Owen said, throwing out his arms with way too much enthusiasm.

Ally did not blame Todd for narrowing his eyes, like he was about to light into Owen.

But Owen barreled on. "Last month I was there to get spaghetti sauce but I kind of lost the money my mom gave me and I knew she'd be really mad because it's possible that's not the first time I lost money she gave me to pick up groceries."

Ally laughed, then covered her mouth, thinking Todd would be angry. But when she snuck a look at him, he was smiling.

"And the other times I just had to go home and get in trouble but your mom said she knew that happened sometimes and she paid for it herself," Owen said. "I brought her the money the next day and she said I was her favorite customer."

And now Todd had a look Ally had never seen before. She wasn't even sure what it was exactly, but looking at Todd now she could tell how much he loved his mom. And to her great surprise, Ally suddenly felt protective of Todd and his mom with the rabbit pin.

But Gemma was clearly feeling differently. "It's not fair that you guys know my secret but I have no idea what you're hiding," she said crossly.

Ally's stomach curdled at that. "Sorry, I really didn't know it was your secret," she said. Ally felt awful she'd been the one to spill about Miles and Gemma.

"Don't you think you should at least tell me yours?" Gemma asked, brushing back a lock of hair that had fallen in her face. "As a fair trade?"

The guilt in Ally hardened instantly because while she'd be willing to do something to make it up to Gemma, she was not revealing her secret for anyone or anything. "No," she said.

"Right, of course not," Gemma muttered, going to stand as far as she could from Ally. "You care more about animals than people, I get it. That's why you don't have any actual human friends."

The words stung and Ally felt her face begin to heat up. She didn't have friends, it was true, but that wasn't her fault. It was stupid Snow Valley not welcoming new people and the fact that Ally worked all the time, and if she cared a lot about animals, well, who could blame her? They were a lot more loyal and forgiving than most people, certainly more so than Gemma herself.

"Todd's right," Ally said as calmly as she could. Her face might be getting red but she was not going to show how much Gemma's remark hurt. "Your secret is a joke. Mine would have an impact on something bigger than just me, same as Todd's. But I get that for someone who only cares about herself, that might not seem important."

Gemma's eyes widened slightly at that and now her face was starting to turn pink. Good, Ally had hurt her back. Though she didn't feel any better.

"We're supposed to be working together, not arguing," Owen said, sounding extremely anxious.

Gemma waved her hand like she could care less and took out her phone. Ally shrugged and tried not to show how close she was to crying.

And then the bell for lunch rang.

GEMMA

Fury burned in Gemma's belly as she threw open the door and stalked down the hall as fast as possible.

Because if she had to spend one more second with anger-management-issues-Todd and backstabbing-Ally both acting like their lives were serious while Gemma's was trivial, well, she was going to really lose it. The worst part was that she had been starting to like both of them. Todd had seemed like a straight shooter and a lot smarter than she'd have guessed while Ally—Ally had seemed like someone Gemma would want to be friends with. Not that this meant Gemma was usually a bad judge of people. Obviously. She had good friends and Miles had chosen her because she was such a good friend. Wasn't there some kind of brainwashing that took place when someone was kidnapped, making the victim start to like their kidnapper? It was probably the same when you were trapped working with people to avoid blackmail.

The hallway was filling up and Gemma slowed down a little, trying to look normal.

"Hey, Gem," Amirah said, coming up with Mei and Bianca. "Sit with us at lunch? There was some major drama with Vivi in our bread-baking group this morning."

All three of them started laughing and Gemma

was overcome with envy. She would have loved being in an Explorer's group with her friends this morning, seeing a juicy drama play out. But of course that would only have happened if Gemma'd had a normal morning with an Explorer's Day class instead of a crime-filled, blackmailed morning with three people she now loathed.

"I can't but definitely tell me everything later," Gemma said, hoping she didn't sound as jealous as she felt.

She dodged a couple of sixth-grade boys who were running and throwing balls of tape at each other and turned the corner. She was now going in the opposite direction of the middle school cafeteria, so there were only a few people, all walking in the opposite direction. The high school also had lunch, in their own cafeteria upstairs, and when possible, Miles snuck down to meet Gemma near the far stairs by the nurse's office, which was closed during lunch. (This had never made sense to Gemma—what if someone choked or threw up during lunch?)

Usually when he missed her at snack, he made it during lunch. But she never knew when he was coming, or if he was coming, because it was hard for him to text. Which totally made sense—he was in high school and very busy. Except, did it make sense? Was he that busy?

Gemma shook her head, irritated with herself. She'd never questioned Miles before and she wasn't going to start now. Ally, Owen, and Todd had poisoned her with their comments, but they had no idea what they were talking about. And obviously high school was busier than middle school—Miles was thinking about colleges already!

Gemma reached the stairs and ducked into the stairwell—one thing she had learned today was that she and Miles had to be more careful, because if Ally had seen them, someone else could too.

Gemma leaned against the wall and crossed her arms over her chest and then admitted to herself that the fights with both Todd and Ally had shaken her. She hadn't meant to insult Todd's mom but clearly he had taken it that way. And why had she said that awful thing to Ally? She hadn't known for sure if Ally had friends until she saw Ally's face cave in at Gemma's remark. It had been mean. Yes, Ally had upset her and been pretty mean herself. But Gemma prided herself on being mature, and the way she'd just acted? Definitely not mature. Not that they didn't both owe her apologies—and it truly wasn't fair that only her secret was known. But still, Gemma wasn't exactly proud of herself.

Gemma heard footsteps and her heart rate picked up with excitement. She smoothed her hair back and adjusted her backpack—but then the footsteps passed. They were too clicky to be Miles anyway—he wore sneakers and had a smooth, almost feathery sound to his steps. Was it weird she knew this? Did he know how her footsteps sounded? No, probably not, because he was pretty much never the one waiting for her. That was because he didn't have to—Gemma was always there and never kept him waiting.

Was that what Ally had meant by a power imbalance?

Gemma gently thumped her head against the wall to get rid of the ridiculous thought. Stupid Ally—what did she know? When Miles got there Gemma was going to prove all three of them wrong by telling him about her day—not that she was being blackmailed, obviously. Or that she'd spent the morning doing some very questionable activities. But she could tell him she was trapped hanging out with a group of people she didn't like and Miles would sympathize and maybe even offer some good advice. Just thinking about it made Gemma smile.

And she was smiling even bigger two minutes later when she heard the smooth, feathery steps of Miles.

"Gemma, awesome, I'm so glad you're here," Miles said, grinning as he slid into the stairwell, smoothing back his hair. He wore a tropical shirt, casually unbuttoned, with a gray t-shirt underneath. His jeans fit well, his hair was styled, and the confident way he rested a hand against the wall while checking to make sure no one had seen him—it was so grown up. A world away from Owen in his grubby athletic pants and Todd in his ill-fitting jeans and old t-shirt.

"I'm glad you're here too," Gemma said. "I had a bad morning."

"Wait 'til you hear about mine," Miles said, grimacing slightly. "It was majorly awful. Remember I told you about that guy Boston, who keeps trying to show me up in gym in front of Coach since we're both going to be trying out for lacrosse in the spring?"

"Right, the one who tripped you when you were running laps last week," Gemma said.

Miles's frown was briefly replaced with a smile just for Gemma. "You're the best, you remember everything," he said.

Gemma beamed. This was what Owen, Ally, and Todd didn't get—Gemma knew how to be a good friend. It wasn't something she worked at, it's just how she was, so while it might seem strange to someone who wasn't that great at being friends, it hadn't surprised Gemma when Miles started talking to her.

"So get what he did today," Miles said, his face turning serious again as he launched into his story.

Gemma nodded and made sympathetic noises like she always did. Miles deserved her full attention, after all. And when he was done she'd tell him about her morning, and she'd get to luxuriate in his attention and sympathy.

Except when Miles was done with that story, he launched into a complaint about the play. "I think Russ has some kind of jealousy issue with me," he began. Gemma nodded because this was not the first time Miles had been upset with Russ, who ran the lighting booth for the play. "We just started blocking and already he's saying I don't need the spotlight during my first monologue and come on, that's why we got the new spotlight, to make this play Broadway big, am I right?"

"Totally," Gemma agreed. "Do you want me to tell Ms. Modi that I couldn't see you very well and maybe the spotlight would help?"

Miles beamed and squeezed her arm. "That would be incredible, thanks."

Gemma's insides fizzed with sweetness, which was how she always felt when she made Miles smile like this. And now he *had* to be ready to listen to her.

But Miles was pulling out his phone. "Okay, gotta go, we don't have the long lunch today that you kids get for Explorer's Day." He leaned over to ruffle Gemma's hair like he so often did. Usually Gemma loved it—it was his way of saying she wasn't really a kid, she was a friend, mature like him. But for some reason it didn't feel that way today. It felt the opposite, like he was proving that she *was* a kid.

"I was hoping I could talk to you about something," she said, shifting her weight.

Miles was back on his phone and apparently hadn't heard her. "Oh, man, I forgot I need to give Ava her chemistry notes back. Talk to you later, Gemma."

And with that he was on his way.

The acidy feeling in her belly was from being hungry, not disappointed, Gemma told herself as she slowly left the stairwell. Miles was busy and he didn't have extended lunch like the middle school. She got that. One hundred percent. And he probably hadn't even heard her say she wanted to talk. If he had, he'd have taken a minute. Because they were friends.

And yet, as she trudged toward the cafeteria, Gemma let herself worry, just for a moment, that maybe they weren't. That maybe, just maybe, Miles talked to her because it was easy, because she never challenged him, because she was fascinated by everything he talked about. And she helped him get the spotlight.

Was that hero worship?

Before Gemma could try to talk herself out of being silly about Miles, she saw James, Owen's obnoxious friend, walking with Ms. Montenegro. James looked angry, Ms. Montenegro looked serious, and neither of them seemed to notice Gemma, who slowed, curious what they were talking about. Not that she was super interested in James or his problems, but why rush to the cafeteria? She'd have to sit with Owen, Todd, and Ally, and Gemma was in no hurry to do that.

But then Gemma heard what Ms. Montenegro said

to James. And the second they'd passed, Gemma was flying to the cafeteria to find the three people who needed to know immediately what had just happened.

TODD

The cafeteria was overwhelmingly loud and the smell of meat loaf, usually one of Todd's favorites, was turning his stomach. His nose had probably been damaged by the pine odor of the stupid janitor's closet. Owen was swiping his card for a full tray of meat loaf and mashed potatoes while Ally, who had already gotten a cheese sandwich, waited for them at the entrance to the seating area. Todd grabbed a bag of salt and vinegar chips in case he got hungry later and stood behind Owen.

"I didn't *want* to tell Mr. Patel that Jane wasn't actually doing the work for our group but really it's on her for expecting the rest of us to get it done while she was doing nothing."

The person behind Todd, whose irritating voice he knew well, had Todd squeezing his chip bag so hard it popped. He turned to glare at Vivi, who had gotten him in trouble more times than he cared to remember, because that was what Vivi lived for: finding people who broke rules and telling on them.

Vivi glared right back. "Go, Todd, it's your turn to swipe your card," she said. "And I want to get through this line before lunch ends."

Todd was slow as possible giving the cashier his lunch card, which made him feel better about how annoying she was.

Then he and Owen followed Ally into the main area where today, and today only, the usual seating system was totally upended. Every other day of the year students sat with friends and the long tables were carefully divided by friend groups and social status. But because many students wanted to keep working on Explorer's Day projects, new groups had formed. Which meant no one looked twice when Todd, who normally sat alone; Owen, who normally sat with his table of idiot friends; and Ally, who Todd had never even seen in the cafeteria, walked to the far end of the room and sat down together. They automatically went to the same table as snack, in a corner by a window and under yet another anti-bullying poster.

Owen picked up his spork and dug into the meat loaf, loading up the bite with mashed potatoes before stuffing it into his mouth. This was how Todd also ate this lunch but he'd never realized it was kind of revolting to watch. Not that it mattered since he ate by himself.

"Aren't you guys hungry?" Owen asked after scarfing up another bite. "I'm starving. I think breaking the law gives me an appetite."

Todd glanced at Ally and when their eyes met, they both laughed.

Ally pulled open the crackly cellophane around her sandwich. "I know I have to eat something but law breaking definitely has the opposite effect on me."

Todd nodded and stuffed the chips in his pocket.

"So we should probably—" Ally began, but then she stopped. She was looking at something behind Todd and when he turned, he saw Gemma hurrying toward them.

"Okay, I know we don't exactly like each other right now," Gemma said, sitting down next to Todd and smoothing back her hair. "But I just heard something and we need to figure out how to work together because it's not good."

Ally squeezed her sandwich so hard the cellophane crunched and the sandwich smushed.

"So it turns out we put that bag of clothes in *James's* locker," Gemma began in a low voice, even though there was no one at the benches near them.

"Wait, you didn't know A-18 was your *friend's* locker?" Todd asked Owen, completely disgusted at Owen's shoddy observation skills.

"I don't know the numbers of my friends' lockers," Owen said in a squeaky voice. "I didn't even know James was in the A alcove 'til right now." He was turning slightly gray. "Gemma, are you sure?"

"Obviously I'm sure or I wouldn't have said it," Gemma said, arching a brow. "I heard him talking about it with Ms. Montenegro when I passed them in the hall. But that's not the bad part."

Owen gripped the edge of the table like he might faint, which seemed like overkill to Todd.

"The bag we put in the locker—it turns out it was clothes James stole from someone in his gym class last month," Gemma went on.

Now Owen appeared to be hyperventilating. "Whose clothes?" he gasped.

"Owen, stop interrupting," Gemma snapped. "I'm

getting to it." Then she looked at him more closely. "Are you okay?"

Owen waved her on.

"Apparently the clothes were stolen from Cody, and Cody had to go down the hall in just his towel to the main office to get something to wear," Gemma said. Owen made a small groaning sound and rested his head on the table. "And thanks to us they found the clothes in James's locker this morning and he confessed that he was the one who did it."

A coldness was beginning to seep through Todd, starting from his core and radiating out.

"Did you know, Owen?" Ally said. Her sandwich was basically a pancake between her palms.

Owen, who looked decidedly ill, shook his head. "No, I'm not in his gym class—he probably did it to be funny and then forgot about it."

"*Cody* didn't forget about it—he left school pretty soon after that, right?" Ally asked.

"Yeah," Gemma said. "Cody was gone two weeks later. James is in major trouble now—someone dropping out because of bullying is serious. But the thing I'm wondering is, if the blackmailer knew James did this, why wait weeks to get him in trouble for it?"

"They were waiting for Explorer's Day, but why?" Ally asked.

Todd had something to say about all this, but suddenly became aware of someone standing just outside his peripheral vision, a little too close to their table for comfort. He whipped his head around and there was Kirby. Not with friends, not with trash to throw away, just Kirby, standing there, looking at their table. And probably listening to them as well.

"What are you doing?" Todd asked him sharply.

Kirby's eyes grew wide when he realized he'd been discovered. "Sorry, I just wanted to ask Owen about basketball practice but I'll come back later." He ducked his head and scurried off, exactly like he had this morning. Todd had thought it was strange then but now it seemed downright suspicious. Especially since wimpy Kirby certainly wasn't on the basketball team. Was *Kirby* the blackmailer?

"What was that about?" Gemma asked, looking after Kirby. "He's not on the team."

"No, he's doing something with stats for a math project," Owen said. His voice sounded hollow—he was really taking the James thing hard. "He asks me about it a lot."

Todd was still concerned Kirby was a threat and was about to say so when Owen leaned forward. "I'm dead," he whispered.

This seemed extreme though Owen did look somewhat corpselike to Todd. Not that he'd seen a dead body outside a TV show or comic but still, Owen was pale in a way that could not be okay.

"If James finds out this is my fault, he'll probably figure out that I'm the one—" Owen broke off and shook his head.

Todd, Ally, and Gemma exchanged a glance.

"Find out what?" Ally asked gently, putting her hand on Owen's arm.

Owen shook his head, gulped, and then shook his head again. Todd was about to get back to the crisis at hand when Owen finally spoke.

"It's my secret," he said, his voice gravelly. "Last month James got suspended for cheating on a test and if he finds out it's my fault—" Owen blinked hard. "None of my friends will ever talk to me again."

"Wait, you sold James out?" Todd asked, surprised given how defensive Owen had gotten about James.

"I didn't mean to," Owen said despairingly. "I was

just talking to Mrs. Fontaine about the test and said something stupid about being able to see the desk in front of you, and she asked me all about it and I kind of let it slip that sometimes people cheat, and then she was really pushing me for names and I admitted James copied off Rosario, and then he got suspended and it never would have come out if I'd just kept my mouth shut."

Yeah, like that ever happened. And it figured Owen's secret was some stupid mess he'd created. Not that Todd didn't feel bad for him—James would definitely make Owen's life miserable over that.

"Owen, if he's really your friend he probably knows you never keep your mouth shut and if you explain it, he'll get it," Gemma said.

Owen looked straight at Gemma. "But the whole 'real friend' thing is complicated, isn't it?"

Todd pressed a hand on the table, ready to intervene if Gemma got mad, because they had to stay focused.

But Gemma sighed and then nodded. "Yeah, it is." She twisted her face ruefully and then smiled at Owen, who smiled back.

"And if James ever finds out I'm the one who put that bag—"

"Okay, about that," Ally began.

But Todd was done waiting. "You guys, this is serious," he said, now pressing both hands on the table. "Before I thought this blackmailer was playing some kind of weird prank or just messing with us, but the fact that she or he found Cody's clothes after James must have thrown them out and came up with this whole plan to expose James?" Todd was suddenly having trouble pulling air into his lungs because the magnitude of this—it was crushing him.

But Ally knew what he was thinking. "The blackmailer waited and planned and gathered what they needed to get James in the worst trouble possible," Ally said. Her fingers were white around the ruined sandwich. "This person is not kidding around. They're out for revenge or something and it's bad—I mean, a bag of clothes that seemed harmless is actually major trouble for James so just imagine what's on that file we put on the principal's computer."

"And what they'll do to us if we don't do everything they tell us," Todd added.

Gemma clenched up her fists, Owen opened and

then closed his mouth, for once at a loss for words, and Ally sagged down in her seat.

"You guys," Gemma said a moment later. "We have to be in the front row of the assembly this afternoon. What is that about?"

Owen shook his head. "Remember that thing about 'stealing the spotlight'? Something big is going to happen if we don't do something to stop it."

"But what can we do?" Gemma asked.

"And what are *they* going to do?" Todd asked, his voice hard.

Ally was squeezing her hands together. "What if they reveal that file and how we were involved?"

Owen sucked in a sharp breath. "Do you think the person is going to tell our secrets at the assembly? I mean, they went to the trouble of finding out what they were so what's to stop them? That would steal the spotlight for sure."

"They wouldn't—they *can't*," Todd said. "My secret— it's not just going to get me in trouble, it could get me arrested."

Both Owen and Gemma looked shocked but it was Ally who spoke.

"Mine too," she said. "Mine too."

OWEN

Owen felt like he was on a roller coaster that had been set to hyper-speed because everything was awful and happening way too fast for his brain to process. Was Todd serious—*arrested*? And Ally? Owen could not imagine Ally doing anything to get herself sent to the principal's office, let alone to prison. Or juvenile hall or wherever twelve-year-old felons had to go.

"Are you sure you're not—" Gemma began.

"No," Todd said firmly and Ally just shook her head.

"Okay," Gemma said, sounding a little like Ally when she used her calm voice. Which Gemma might have actually been imitating. "I think it's time you told us what happened."

Ally's eyes filled with tears and she pressed her fist against her mouth.

Todd was staring down at his hands on the table but then he shrugged. "Since it probably won't stay a secret for much longer, I guess it doesn't matter if you know. I forge my grandfather's signature on social security checks and put them in my mom's bank account."

Owen sat very still. He could hear people laughing, talking, trays clanking on the dish return, and someone getting yelled at for not recycling a bottle. So his ears still worked—but he could not have heard Todd correctly. Forgery? Stealing from his own grandfather? Todd was right—this was going to get him locked up.

"Um, so I'm guessing you had a reason?" Gemma asked. She was blinking a lot but still using the calm voice.

Todd began rubbing the table with his thumb. "During Covid Mom's hours got cut and even though she got that essential workers' pay bump, the store wasn't open twenty-four hours anymore and they didn't need as many cashiers, so she was only working part-time and it wasn't enough. For anything—food, rent on the trailer, even electricity."

Todd's voice got lower. "This one night our electricity was cut off and our food was going to go bad and it was super hot in the trailer and Mom—she just, she couldn't stop crying. So I said I'd take care of it. We'd been getting my grandfather's checks—he took off a few years ago, I have no idea where—and before I'd just been throwing them out but when the next one came, I signed it and deposited it and told Mom I got a part-time job too."

"Oh, Todd," Gemma said. "That must have been—"

"So scary!" Owen cut in. "I can't believe your electricity went off—they shouldn't be allowed to do that."

Todd laughed a hard, very not funny, laugh. "Yeah, right. But it wasn't just that—Mom was worried if she couldn't support us that I'd get taken away."

That seemed insane to Owen but Gemma was nodding. "She might have been right. You were smart to do what you did."

Owen was shocked but Todd looked like he was about to have a heart attack from surprise. "Really?" he asked, looking at Gemma like she was one of the giant squid from *Watchmen*.

"Yeah, I mean, getting benefits during Covid took forever and a lot of people didn't get them and it doesn't sound like your mom was in shape to apply for anything," Gemma said, and she sounded herself again. "Plus offices here in town were closed, so she'd have had to go to Albany and what if they were closed there too? And if they were open was it even safe to go?" Gemma nodded. "You did the right thing—the only thing, really."

Todd let out a shaky breath. "Thanks," he said. "I'm not sure anyone else will see it that way, but—"

"I do," Owen said.

"I do too," Ally said. Her eyes were still red but she was no longer teary. "I also get why you're scared. You did the right thing but you had to break the law to do it."

Owen's brain felt slightly less like exploding when Ally put it that way. And it made sense—as Gemma said, there hadn't exactly been a lot of options for Todd and his mom. Though Owen couldn't help thinking it was pretty rough that Todd had had to be the one to take care of his mom. But picturing Todd's mom now, her shaky smile and rabbit pin—well, it wasn't that hard to imagine her crying like Todd had described. Owen wasn't sure why exactly, but it was as if she was made of something a bit more fragile than Todd. Or Owen's mom. His mom handled everything—she was an accountant and had immediately taken on extra work when Covid hit. She and Big Rob were worried about things like retirement and college funds but they'd certainly never been close to having their electricity turned off. At least not that Owen was aware of. And he suddenly realized how lucky that was, not having to worry about things like that, the way Todd did.

"So did you have to break a law to do the right thing too?" Todd asked Ally.

Owen braced himself on the uncomfortable cafeteria bench because he had the feeling Ally's secret was going to be even harder to process.

"Yeah, pretty much," Ally said, looking down. Her hands were in her lap and she was twisting at the cuff of her sweatshirt. "Mine was during the Covid shutdown too. I was out for a walk, and a little ways outside town I passed this house with a dog tied out back—like tied with rope. The yard was all muddy and the dog had a lame paw and was too thin—you could see it all the way from the road. And the rope was short and I just couldn't not do something."

"I don't blame you," Todd said, anger in his voice. "Those people should have been the ones going to jail for that."

"So yeah, that's the thing," Ally said looking up. "I went back late at night and took the dog and brought her to the sanctuary and, yes, it was the right thing to save her, but I'm not like you—there were other things I could have done. *Should* have done, really."

"Like what?" Owen asked. It turned out that Ally's secret did not blow him away after all—it actually made a lot of sense. He could even imagine himself doing the same thing if he'd seen something like that. And lived in an animal sanctuary instead of in a house with a parent allergic to dogs. But still, it could get Ally and maybe even the sanctuary in a lot of trouble.

"I should have called the police or animal services," Ally said. "They know my family and would have looked into it."

"So why didn't you?" Gemma asked. She was playing absently with her hair, twining it around her fingers.

"I was worried that because of social distancing restrictions it might take a while for them to be able to look into or harder to get the family to let them in and that the dog—Buttons—might not make it," Ally said. "But I should have at least looked into it or asked my grandparents before basically stealing her."

"Rescuing her," Todd corrected.

Ally nodded. "Yeah, at the time it felt like I had no

choice—I had to get her out of there as fast as possible to save her life. But if it gets out and anyone finds out I not only stole Buttons but kept her at the sanctuary—" Her eyes filled with tears.

"We're not going to let anyone find out," Gemma said so fiercely Owen jumped. "We're going to find out who's blackmailing us and stop whatever they have planned—no one is going to spill any of our secrets or do something to hurt any one of us, not if I have anything to say about it."

Owen's spirits lifted at this.

"We've been trying all day to figure out this person's plan and who they are and we came up with nothing," Ally said, glancing at the clock. "Now we only have an hour before the assembly."

This dampened Owen's spirits because everything Ally said was true.

Todd let his head fall into his hands. "There's nothing we can do to stop whatever this person has planned," he said, his voice muffled. "It's impossible— they've already won."

"Nothing is impossible," Gemma said. "We just have to figure out a strategy."

"Like what?" Ally asked.

Despite her brave words, Gemma said nothing. In the pause, Owen could hear that people were gathering up their things. The bell that ended their extended lunch was going to ring soon, and they had no plan.

"Actually I have an idea," Owen said hesitantly. He thought his idea was pretty good but what if it was stupid? It wouldn't be the first time that had happened.

But they were all looking at him, even Todd, who had picked up his head, so Owen went on. "Okay, so you know how in English when we were writing mysteries Ms. Brier said that thing about how you have to read your story out loud and go through everything step by step to make sure you don't have any plot holes?"

Todd opened his mouth but Gemma put a hand on his arm. "Let Owen finish," she said.

"Okay, so when I did it for class it helped me see a bunch of things in my story that I hadn't noticed before. And I saw how I could string things together a lot better so that my clues made sense. Ms. Brier even said it was the best thing I'd written for the class."

"So you want us to write the story of what happened today?" Todd asked impatiently.

A group of eighth graders passed by their table as Owen shook his head. "No," he said softly when the kids had passed. "I'm thinking if we make a recording going through every detail of what happened and then listened to it, maybe we'd see clues that were there in plain sight but we missed them because at the time everything happened so fast."

Todd was silent but Gemma was nodding. "That makes sense."

"In TV shows they make those boards of suspects and go over the backstory all the time," Owen added, excited she liked his idea. "It's like an audio version of that."

"I think they do that so the person watching doesn't forget all the suspects," Todd said. "But still, it's not a bad idea."

"And it's our only idea," Ally added as the bell rang.

"Let's do it," Gemma said. "Because we are not going down without a fight."

CHAPTER 7

RECORDING PART 6

GEMMA: So that's the question: Who is the blackmailer?

OWEN: We're almost done talking about all the steps and I still have no idea. Sorry, guys. Making this recording was a waste of time.

ALLY: Not necessarily. I mean, going over everything helped me remember some of the details I'd missed or forgotten.

TODD: But do any of them tell you who's behind this?

ALLY: No, but maybe they can tell us why—like why did this person make a whole plan to get James in trouble? Who hates James?

TODD: Cody.

GEMMA: Right but he can't be the blackmailer—the blackmailer was here today to hide the flash drive and stuff. Cody's in Virginia.

OWEN: Maryland.

TODD: Owen knows—he's friends with Cody.

OWEN: No, he got weird during Covid so I stopped hanging out with him. That might be another reason his sister doesn't like me.

ALLY: How was he weird?

OWEN: He was on his computer all the time. I mean, we all were, I know, but he wasn't doing normal stuff like gaming or watching dumb videos. He was doing some research project.

ALLY: That doesn't sound weird.

GEMMA: No, Owen's right, he was weird. He asked me

to go with him to movie night wearing a minion mask. I mean, yes, the movie was *Minions* but still, that's weird.

TODD: So you shut him down.

GEMMA: Well, yes, but nicely. I didn't tell him I thought he was weird, I just said I had other plans. And this doesn't have anything to do with our list. We need to figure out who else hates James.

TODD: That's a long list and you can put me on it. But whoever set up James also hates us—I mean, they found out all our secrets to blackmail us into doing all this. Who would have it out for the four of us too?

[*Silence.*]

OWEN: I say we start with a list of people who don't like James and then see who on that list might have a reason to be after us too.

GEMMA: Yeah, the James list will be long so we'll have a lot of choices.

OWEN: He's not that bad!

[*Chorus of disagreement from the others.*]

Okay, whatever, let's just make the list. Henry Chang hates him because James told Henry that it's his fault Covid came from China to America.

GEMMA: Henry's Korean American and he grew up here—the virus had nothing to do with him!

ALLY: It didn't have anything to do with Chinese Americans either—people blaming random Asian people for the virus are racist idiots. James really is a jerk.

OWEN: I did tell him it was racist and some of the other guys did too. And he stopped.

GEMMA: Good.

OWEN: We should put Leo on too. James took his spot on the basketball team. It's possible James lied to Leo about a practice time, which is why Leo lost the spot. I know—don't yell at me—it was a mean thing to do.

GEMMA: And you actually like this guy? Wait, don't answer, I'll just lose all respect for you. So do any of you guys have beef with Henry or Leo? I mean, they probably don't like Owen because he hangs out with James.

OWEN: It never used to bother Leo but I don't know—now that I'm thinking about it, it's been a while since he waited for me to walk to school. And remember how he was weird at lunch? That could mean something.

GEMMA: Yeah, that's right! He was acting as if he had something to hide.

ALLY: Like blackmail! But does he have a problem with all of us?

TODD: Henry and I had a situation last year when he bumped into me in the hall. And actually I had a thing with Leo when we were doing a social studies project together.

ALLY: Did you punch him?

TODD: I already told you I don't remember—but if I did it was a while ago.

GEMMA: I'm starting to think you might have as many people who don't like you as James, no offense.

TODD: It's not my fault so many people here are annoying.

GEMMA: That's one way of looking at it, but let's focus—Ally, have you had any issues with Henry or Leo? I've never had a problem with Henry but I ran up points on Leo when we had mixed team scrimmage last year so I might not be his favorite person.

ALLY: Henry and I sometimes talk in math class—no issues there. I think Leo got mad at me when I contradicted him in class at the beginning of the year—but he was wrong! I'm not sure if he's the kind of guy to hold a grudge.

OWEN: Let's assume he is. If he's had issues with all of us, plus he's acting strange, he's a suspect.

ALLY: Great. Okay, who else has it in for James?

TODD: What about Kirby? He's been really jumpy today and he was lurking around our table at lunch.

OWEN: Kirby and James are cousins, so no.

ALLY: Just because they're related doesn't mean they like each other. And that could explain how the blackmailer found the bag of clothes—James probably took them home.

GEMMA: No, I heard James tell Ms. Montenegro he left them in the garbage can by the gym. So anyone could have found them.

OWEN: And Kirby and James are tight—they hang out a lot and have all these inside jokes about their family.

GEMMA: Okay, so Kirby's out but I just thought of someone who has it in for everybody: Vivi.

[*Several voices agreeing.*]

OWEN: That is such a good call: Vivi lives to get people in trouble.

ALLY: I've definitely seen her rat people out, and she doesn't like me at all, but would she actually blackmail us?

OTHER THREE: Yes!

ALLY: Okay, okay—so Vivi and Leo are our top suspects.

GEMMA: I say we start investigating them as soon as the bell rings.

TODD: How are we going to do that?

OWEN: Go talk to them and see if they act suspicious— and then if they do, try and get them to confess.

GEMMA: [*Slight muffled sound.*] I'm going to look them both up too—I know Vivi has social media accounts so maybe she's posted something that would give her away.

TODD: Like what? "Here's a selfie of me dumpster div- ing for Cody's clothes"?

[*Laughter.*]

GEMMA: Maybe not quite that obvious but some kind of clue that she's planning something devious or has it out for James or whatever. [*Pause.*] I'm not seeing much besides posts like "my perfect math test" and "look who got the good citizen's certificate for September."

OWEN: Barf.

GEMMA: Yeah. And Leo doesn't have an account at all.

TODD: [*In a low voice.*] We're going to find out who's behind this and stop them, right? Because if we don't . . .

GEMMA: Yes, we are. We're the ones stealing the spotlight now—stealing it from the blackmailer. We have ten minutes until the bell—let's listen to this recording, find out hidden clues, and get this handled.

MONDAY: 1:22 P.M.
TODD

Todd cracked open the closet door and peeked out, then all four of them hurried into the hall. Hiding out in the janitor's closet was pretty minor compared with other things they'd done today, but he didn't want to get caught for it. Students burst into the hall as classrooms emptied, and there was a festive feeling in the air. The Showcases were fun—everyone liked the walk-through to see what other groups had done, even if it was just jars of unusual vegetables being pickled or a set of completed puzzles. And the Explorer's Day assembly after that was like a party celebrating the day, with everyone hoping they'd be in the PowerPoint picture teachers took showing each group's "learning process."

"Hey, Owen," Erlan, a kid who reported for the school paper, said, coming up to them. Being around this many people felt weird to Todd after all the time in the closet. "I hear your friend James is in trouble."

"Matt told me he's getting suspended for a week," said Khai, who was an impressive skateboarder. He sounded happy about this and Todd decided maybe some of the guys Owen knew were okay. It was possible just the basketball guys were the total jerks.

"I haven't really talked to him today," Owen said.

They all stepped to the side as a group of girls hurried past.

"If he was the one who stole those clothes, then he had it coming," Erlan said. "I was in that gym class and Cody walking down the hall in a towel was bad."

"James should have been suspended longer," Todd said.

Khai looked slightly surprised to have Todd join the conversation but then he nodded. "Yeah, it's not the first obnoxious thing he's done."

"And it won't be the last," Todd agreed.

Both Erlan and Khai nodded as they walked ahead to join some girls from their class.

"Maybe they should be suspects since they don't like James," Ally said.

"No, they just know a bully when they see one," Gemma said. "Unlike Owen."

"A lot of people like James," Owen protested, but his voice was kind of feeble.

Todd officially admired how blunt Gemma was. And the fact that she thought he'd done the right thing signing the checks—well, no one could change that it was illegal and could get Todd, and Mom, in awful trouble. But still, it felt good to have her say it. Though admitting what he'd done had left him feeling a little wobbly. Not bad wobbly exactly, more that a place inside him that had been armored over was now a bit Jell-O-like.

The crowd was getting thicker as they came close

to the gym, where teachers and a few student volunteers were inside setting up the Showcases. Everyone was supposed to get in "an orderly line" while waiting for the doors to open. But considering there were only a few teachers in the hall with all three middle school grades, it was not exactly orderly.

"Okay, we know what we're doing and where we're meeting up, so let's get this done," Gemma said quietly, stopping behind a group of gamer-type sixth graders. Listening to the recording had not helped but they still had two prime suspects, as Owen called them. So the plan was for the boys to find Leo and the girls to track down Vivi.

"Sounds good," Todd said, ready to finally go do something about the maniac trying to destroy his life. Ally grabbed his arm.

"Be subtle," she said. "If it's him, we don't want him to know we're onto him—we need evidence so we have some power."

Normally Todd would have snapped at anyone telling him something so obvious, but hearing Ally's secret, how she'd risked so much to save a dog because it was the right thing to do—it had Todd deciding he wasn't going to snap at her for a while. Maybe not ever. So instead he just nodded.

"Right, we'll be totally stealth," Owen said, bouncing on his toes as he craned his neck looking for Leo.

"That means *not* advertising that you want to find someone," Todd pointed out. He gave Ally and Gemma a thumbs-up as they slipped through the crowd toward the gym doors. A kiss-up like Vivi was bound to be in the front.

"Got it," Owen said. He was still looking around but at least he'd stopped bouncing.

"All right people, let's take it down a notch or we're all going home today with headaches," Nurse Simmons called out. She was kind of a hypochondriac, always thinking kids had things like TB instead of a cold, but Todd thought she had a point today. Clearly no one else did though because the noise level remained the same.

"Hey, Owen," Dev said, turning around and noticing them. "What group are you in?" He glanced at Todd. "Um, you guys."

Todd was ready to tell him to mind his own business but Owen mumbled something in a low voice. And before Dev could ask him to repeat it, Owen spoke up louder. "What about you?"

"D&D with Ms. Dunbar," he said. "I made an amazing character—he's half elf, half demon."

"Cool," Owen said. "I think Leo's in that one too, right?"

Todd could not help being impressed with this bit of slick detective work on Owen's part.

"No, Leo's in nutrition," Dev said, his nose wrinkling slightly. "Don't ask me why anyone would choose that."

Todd and Owen both laughed.

"All right folks, we're opening the doors. Let's keep it orderly," Nurse Simmons called above the crowd noise.

There was a slow push toward the gym, the sound of the doors banging open, and someone shouting about a lost water bottle. Todd looked both ways down the hall but couldn't pick out Leo in the mass of people. It didn't help that Leo was pretty blah-looking.

"Do you see him?" he asked Owen.

Owen shook his head and Todd clenched his fists because once they got in the gym there wouldn't be any switching spots. The teachers inside would be serious about keeping people in line and moving past each showcase at an even pace.

"I think—" Owen began, and Todd looked eagerly in the direction Owen was squinting, but then Owen said, "No, that's not him."

Todd was starting to heat up in the packed space and his lungs felt tight. Where was stupid Leo? Why was this so badly organized? What if—

"There he is," Owen said, "coming around the corner with Chloe and Vaughn."

Yes! Todd felt his body relax now that their target had been spotted. Owen set off toward Leo and Todd followed. Since no one liked Todd it made sense for Owen to be in charge of the actual conversation.

"Boys, get in line." Nurse Simmons had come up behind them.

"Sorry, we got separated from our group and we're just going to meet them," Todd said, impressed by his own smooth cover. Unfortunately his excuse didn't seem to be as effective—Nurse Simmons was looking at him like he'd been taken over by aliens. The "sorry" had probably been too much, given the troubled history between Todd and the nurse. But then she caught sight of someone getting shoved, right into an anti-bullying poster, and hurried over.

Owen grabbed Todd's arm and they headed toward Leo.

ALLY

The crowd was even more packed closer to the gym, and Ally was working hard not to lose Gemma, when she suddenly felt a hand on her back. A moment later she was officially being pushed out of the way by a very obnoxious eighth grader.

"Watch it," Ally said sharply.

"Get out of the way, then," the guy said.

"I don't like how you're talking to my friend," Gemma said. "Back off."

"Whatever," the guy said, throwing up his hands. But he moved more carefully this time.

"Nicely handled," Gemma said, now following in the guy's wake because they still hadn't found Vivi.

"My grandma always says, 'A lady must stand up for her dignity at all times,'" Ally said.

Gemma grinned. "I like that a lot."

It gave Ally a warm feeling to hear Gemma

appreciate Grandma's words. It had been a long time, but Ally did remember that this was what it felt like to have a friend. Not that Gemma was a *real* friend of course—after today she'd go back to her busy life and Ally would go back to, well, being busy outside school. But still, it felt good today.

Especially since Gemma knew her secret. Saying it out loud had been a lot of things actually. Scary but also kind of a relief. It got her reliving how infuriating it had been seeing Buttons so neglected, and how wonderful it was watching her slowly start to trust people, gain weight while her paw healed, and play with other dogs. But then there had been the lying to her grandparents about how she'd just found Buttons left on the edge of the sanctuary. And the horrible guilt, like a ball of wet newspaper in her gut, of knowing she had put the sanctuary in jeopardy. Saying it all out loud did not make that better.

"I don't see Vivi," Gemma said, looking around, a frown on her face, bringing Ally back to the matter at hand. They had finally reached the front of the crowd. The students were even more densely packed here by the still-closed gym doors, but Vivi, who was tall and had bright red hair, generally stood out no matter how big the group. Time was running out! They *had* to find Vivi before the assembly.

"Maybe she's in the back?" Gemma asked. They both knew this was not likely—the kids who were teacher pleasers always went up front. Unless—

"Wait, I bet she's one of the student volunteers helping out inside," Ally exclaimed. Each table had a few volunteers to explain the display and hand out any food samples.

"Oh, of course," Gemma said. "That won't give us much time to try and talk to her though."

This was true and a big problem.

"Gemma," someone called out behind them. A girl named Mei, who Ally knew was on the basketball team, squeezed her way beside them.

"Hey, Mei," Gemma said, clearly happy to see her. Ally sighed a little.

"So let me tell you what happened in our group this morning," Mei said, stopping with her back to Ally. She hadn't even seemed to notice her. Ally took a step back so that she wouldn't intrude on their conversation, but then Gemma took her arm.

"I want to hear everything but first, do you know Ally? We've been hanging out today," Gemma said.

The warmth in Ally's stomach bloomed through her whole body as she smiled at Mei. "We have science together," she said.

Mei nodded. She was wearing her practice jersey and her long hair was up in a high ponytail. "I cracked up the other day when you told Mr. Salvatore that pigs are more intelligent than dogs."

Ally smiled. "I love dogs but pigs really are smarter."

"I looked it up later and it's kind of amazing how smart they are," Mei said, twirling the end of her ponytail and nearly hitting Ally in the face. They were all definitely standing a little too close, which was probably some kind of fire hazard.

"So the bread-baking drama," Gemma prompted.

Ally didn't get why Gemma was so interested in some story from bread baking when they needed to be figuring out how to get to Vivi.

"Right," Mei said. "You know how Vivi is really mean but she never shows that in front of teachers?"

A jolt of electricity went through Ally because some intel about Vivi was exactly what they needed. Gemma was a genius for asking about this drama!

"Yes, totally," Gemma said.

"Okay, so—"

But then one of the gym doors opened, and people pushed forward. Mei bumped into Ally while Gemma had to grab the boy next to her to keep from stumbling.

"You could get killed in this crowd," Mei complained, which was an exaggeration though maybe not much of one.

"Folks, it's time to begin our Showcase," Coach Tiffins called in a booming voice. "No pushing— everyone will get in and see every showcase. We'll be counting you off in groups of ten and directing you to a spot. Once you are all in place, we'll begin."

"So what happened?" Gemma asked, leaning toward Mei. She was so close to Ally that Ally could feel Gemma's breath on her arm.

Mei lit up in anticipation of sharing what was clearly a juicy story. "Mr. Patel brought—"

Coach Tiffins was suddenly looming over them and Ally realized they'd made it to the gym doors. "Ladies, the three of you are over the group limit— someone will have to wait for the next set of ten."

Ally shot Gemma a desperate look, but Mei was Gemma's friend so Ally knew who had to stay back. She stood with a group of sixth-grade boys talking about Minecraft and watched Gemma head inside without her.

OWEN

Owen tried not to bump into anyone as he and Todd made their way toward Leo. It was hard because everyone else was going the other way so no one was looking very carefully at where they were going.

"Sorry," Eric said to Todd, after nearly running into him.

Todd glared at him, and Eric, who was a big guy, cowered a little. "My bad," he said.

Todd shook his head in disgust as Eric slunk away. It was nearly impossible for Owen to imagine Todd— gruff, tough, hard-edged Todd, taking care of his fragile mom with the rabbit pin. And then figuring out a way to save them from eviction and child services. That was the kind of thing a comic book hero would do. A really cool hero. How was it that Todd had kept that Todd, hero-Todd, hidden away for so long?

"Keep going," Todd snapped, poking Owen in the back. Well, however he had done it, he was good at it.

Owen walked around a group of girls taking a not-so-secret selfie, and then up to Leo, Chloe, and Vaughn.

"Hey," Owen said, trying to sound casual. He gave his neighbor a quick once-over to see if he looked suspicious but it was kind of hard to tell. Leo just looked like Leo.

"So Leo, we were talking to Dev and he said you were in the nutrition Explorer's group and I wanted to ask about it," Owen went on.

Leo's brows scrunched up. "Why? You told me it sounded like the most boring group ever when the Explorer's list came out last month."

Had Owen said that? It was likely.

"Right, yeah," Owen improvised quickly. "But a few days ago I got this bad stomachache so I think I should learn more about it."

"You get Doritos and M&Ms every snack," Leo said. "That's why you got a stomachache."

Todd snickered and even Chloe was smiling.

"And weren't you the one who got five ice cream sandwiches for lunch last week?" Vaughn asked unhelpfully. "Everyone in my math class was talking about it and how you ate them really fast and managed not to puke."

Only a lightweight would be unable to handle a measly five ice cream sandwiches but Owen took inspiration from his graphic novel character's spy stealth and simply nodded. "Yeah, but see, I think that's the problem—I might have a sugar addiction," he said. "And a Dorito addiction too."

Todd was snickering again but Leo, Vaughn, and Chloe were all nodding. The crowd of students was now moving slowly toward the gym and Owen made sure to stay close to Leo. It was hard because Leo kept trying to wait for Vaughn and Chloe, but Owen, like his graphic novel character, was persistent. If Leo had anything to do with the blackmailing, Owen was going to find out.

"My mom's a nurse and she says it can be challenging to break certain patterns of eating," Chloe said. "We eat stuff because it's familiar."

"And not because it just tastes good?" Todd asked skeptically.

Owen paused so he could step on Todd's foot to get him to shut up.

But Chloe just laughed. "That too, of course. And we learned some cool stuff in nutrition."

"Yeah, like about how smart it is to start every day by eating some protein," Leo said enthusiastically.

"Wow," Owen said, already bored.

Leo gave him a skeptical glance. "See, you could care less about this."

Yikes, maybe he needed to work on his stealth skills—Leo had seen right through him.

"What group were you guys in?" Vaughn asked politely.

This was not what Owen wanted to talk about at all. He was trying to come up with an answer to get things back on track when the line moved forward and Todd crashed into Leo.

"Sorry," Todd said, not sounding sorry at all. "I'm just excited to get inside because one of the groups did a study on keeping secrets and I want to see the results."

It was clumsy but Owen had to admit it was smart: Catch Leo off guard, see if he looked guilty. Unfortunately Leo still just looked like Leo, at least to Owen.

"I'm really good at keeping secrets," Chloe said

cheerfully. They had rounded the corner and Owen could see the gym filling up in front of them.

"I'm not," Leo said, sounding a bit sad about it. Or was this an elaborate fake-out to fool Owen and Todd? "I ruined my brother's surprise birthday party last year and he's still mad at me about it."

Had Owen known this? It was possible. Sometimes on the way to school Leo went on about stuff and Owen stopped listening.

Vaughn laughed. "I remember that," he said. "Your mom was mad too."

"Yeah, she still calls me Loose Lips," Leo said, smiling and shaking his head. "But I always forget what I'm not supposed to talk about and blurt it out."

"Tell me about it," Vaughn said. "Remember when—"

"Don't bring up the time—"

"You told my dad I was the one who broke the screen door with my hockey stick," Vaughn finished.

Leo sighed. "It was a mistake, okay? I already said I was sorry."

Owen looked at Todd, who was clearly thinking the same thing he was: Loose Lips Leo was not their guy.

So now they could only hope that the girls were

having better luck with Vivi. Because if not, they were in trouble.

GEMMA

Gemma felt bad ditching Ally but the clock was ticking down—they only had half an hour left to find out if Vivi was the one blackmailing them. So Gemma walked next to Mei into the gym that was set up with rows of tables holding displays from all the Explorer's Day classes.

"Okay, I think I can finally tell you the story," Mei said. She and Gemma stood toward the back of their group at the drawing class's display. "And is it me or does it smell like wet dog in here?" She wrinkled her nose.

"It's not you, it always smells like wet dog in here," Gemma answered. "And I'm so ready to hear what happened."

"Okay, so we were divided up into types of bread and Vivi was in the sourdough group, which I thought sounded great because I love sourdough," Mei said. "And I was in whole wheat, which is so not as good. But it turns out sourdough needs this disgusting goop called a starter—it's like white slime."

Gemma nodded, trying to ignore the two boys in the group who were bored and trying to see who could burp loudest. What was it with boys and burping?

"Evie was in the group and she gets the starter from Mr. Patel, but then Vivi tries to take it from her, because you know Vivi and how she has to be in charge of everything."

Both girls rolled their eyes at this annoying truth.

"Folks, time to move on," Coach Tiffins thundered across the gym. Gemma jumped.

"You seem tense," Mei said, touching her arm.

"Um, maybe a little," Gemma said as they followed their group over to the next showcase, which was D&D. "But I'm fine—go on."

"Right, okay, so Vivi grabs it and Kate decides she's not letting go, and then the starter spills all over Vivi," Mei said, clearly delighted. It *was* a delightful image.

"And, listen, that stuff was gross, but the way Vivi freaked out you'd have thought it was nuclear waste," Mei said. "She was screaming at Kate, calling her a clumsy idiot, and Mr. Patel rushed over, saying it was an accident and not a big deal, and then Vivi yelled at *him*!"

"She yelled at a teacher?" Gemma asked, shocked.

"Okay, maybe not actual yelling, but definitely talking back. She said it was a big deal in this rude way, and Mr. Patel told her she needed to sit down and get a hold of herself," Mei went on.

Vivi acting so out of character—it had to mean *something*. Maybe that something was her high stress level because she was running a secret blackmail scheme today?

"I've never seen Mr. Patel have to talk to a student like that," Mei said.

"Everybody loves him," Gemma said, eager to get back to Vivi. "Only Vivi is evil enough to get in trouble with him."

"Oh, but actually there was that weird thing with Cody," Mei said. "Were we in the same world history class last year?"

Gemma shook her head and tried not to let her impatience show—she was not interested in something that happened last year.

"Mr. Patel thought Cody was cheating and Cody

got really upset—he actually *was* yelling and had to go to the office and everything," Mei said, absently twirling the end of her ponytail. "It was just a mis-understanding but Cody totally lost it and Mr. Patel was angry—it was so weird because he never gets angry. And we were all telling Cody to shut up because, come on, who yells at Mr. Patel?"

"Seriously," Gemma said. "I can't believe Vivi was even rude to him today." It was a weak connection but she was desperate to get back to the story.

"Vivi didn't actually yell though, not like Cody," Mei said. Their group was being shuffled to puzzle mania. "And she apologized right away."

Gemma nodded, waiting, but Mei was now mov-ing closer to the puzzle table, clearly interested in the display of 3-D puzzles.

"So then what happened?" Gemma asked.

"That was basically it," Mei said.

Disappointment hit Gemma hard. While hearing about Vivi disgracing herself was enjoyable, and snap-ping at Mr. Patel could indicate stress, that wasn't real evidence.

"Hm," she said, trying to seem casual and see if

maybe Mei would remember something—anything!— else. "You know, I saw Vivi this morning and she didn't look like a mess."

"Oh, she left to go change into her gym clothes," Mei said, leaning down to check out the puzzle that was one thousand solid red pieces. "How did someone do this?"

But Gemma's mind was far from the puzzles. Because if Vivi had left the classroom she could have used that time to place the clothes under the dumpster or hide the items in Ms. Piedmont's room! Or both!

"When she came back she said that it had been a challenging couple of weeks but today all her hard work was going to pay off," Mei said, straightening up. "And that was the end of it."

Gemma stood very, very still. "Vivi said that today her hard work was going to pay off?"

"Yeah," Mei said. "Strange, right?"

Gemma nodded. This was not just strange—*this* was real evidence. Vivi was the one blackmailing them!

CHAPTER 8

MONDAY: 1:58 P.M.
TODD

"Hurry," Todd hissed at Gemma, Owen, and Ally as they headed down the hall to the auditorium. He and Owen had met up with the girls after Showcases ended. Todd had been angry the Leo lead was a bust, but now that Vivi was suspect number one he was revved up and ready.

"We are," Gemma said, just as Owen walked into Todd.

"I said hurry, not run me over," Todd snapped. What was wrong with these people? They had five minutes before the assembly would begin and couldn't even walk down the hall without problems.

"Sorry," Owen said. "I was looking—"

"Walk in front of me," Todd told him irritably.

"Just trying to find you-know-who," Owen said. Like that was a stealth thing to say. Owen was ridiculous.

They joined the stream of students walking through the doors of the auditorium and Todd looked around the big room. The rows of wooden seats were glowing in the sunlight pouring in the windows that covered one wall. The other walls were of course covered with Gold Star and anti-bullying posters, and a few playbills from past drama club productions.

"She's over there," Ally said, gripping Todd's wrist.

"Where?" Todd turned quickly to see if Vivi was behind them.

"Across from us, near the stage," Ally said in a quiet voice. "I think she's going to sit in the front row too."

Sure enough Vivi and her friend Sophia were on the opposite side of the auditorium and turning to sit in the very first row of seats.

Vivi looked up suddenly. Caught staring, Todd froze. She glared at him, then leaned to say something to Sophia, her eyes still on Todd as her lip curled. Every muscle in Todd's body stiffened because Vivi looked exactly like a comic archvillain. And she "just happened" to be in a place where she could observe Todd and the others in the front row. Plus no one loved the spotlight more than Vivi. Gemma was right: Vivi had to be the blackmailer. And they had three and a half minutes to stop whatever she was planning at the assembly.

Todd began shoving his way through the crowd, not caring if the others followed. He could take it from here. The best route was to get to the front of the auditorium, cross the aisle by the stage, and confront Vivi. Todd managed to get to the front, with the other three impressively right behind him, but a group of sixth graders was blocking the aisle and as Todd pushed past them he stepped on someone's foot.

"Ow!" the guy screamed, as if Todd had severed his foot, not just put a little pressure on it.

"Relax," Todd snapped.

"That hurt," the kid wailed, his voice shrill. Why did he have to be so loud? He was going to get Todd in—

"Mr. Hanley, is there a problem?" Coach Tiffins asked, coming up to them easily as the sea of people suddenly parted. No one wanted to block the coach.

"No sir, we're all fine," Todd said, glaring at the kid.

But the boy was looking at Coach Tiffins and missed Todd's clear message. "I'm not okay," he told the coach. "That guy stepped on my foot and it really hurt."

"I said I was sorry," Todd said sharply.

And the kid finally got it, probably because one of his friends poked him so hard he nearly fell over.

"Sure, yeah, it's okay," the kid told Coach Tiffins.

"I'm glad," the coach said, in a voice that made it clear he was not glad and did not believe the kid. Or Todd. "Mr. Hanley, why don't you have a seat?"

Todd looked despairingly across the auditorium at Vivi. She was so close! "Actually, I—" Todd began, but then the coach put his hand on Todd's shoulder and steered him to a seat in the front row.

"I think this will do nicely," the coach said, practically forcing Todd down. Todd hit the seat so hard he felt it vibrate up his spine. Todd looked at Gemma hovering behind Coach Tiffins, who was fully blocking the aisle. She was their last hope.

But then Todd heard it—the sound of feedback through the microphone. Principal Grace was up on the stage and the assembly was starting. Gemma sat down three seats from Todd, Owen sat next to her, and Ally sank down next to Todd. He could see she was blinking back tears. And who could blame her?

They had failed to find the blackmailer and now they were going to be destroyed.

OWEN

Owen sagged in his seat as Principal Grace tapped the microphone. Ms. Montenegro stood next to him and Ms. Atkins was sitting by the laptop that had the PowerPoint of all the Explorer's Day "learning processes." Each group had selected one person to present a quick summary of their work, accompanied by a PowerPoint picture montage projected up on the huge screen.

"Hello, Explorers!" Principal Grace shouted. "I'm thrilled to be able to celebrate the incredible learning that has taken place here today. The students of Snow Valley Secondary's middle school are some of the top students in the country! Which is why we won the Gold Star Award last year, and why we might just win it again, putting the spotlight on our school once more!" He gestured to the lighting booth, in case anyone had missed the reference to the new addition.

Acid was crawling up Owen's throat and the reference to the spotlight did not help. Waiting, knowing the axe was going to fall but not knowing when, was torture. Next to him Ally sniffed loudly. On his other side Gemma was gripping her armrests, her face tense.

"I want to take a moment to remind everyone of the success of our anti-bullying campaign," Principal Grace went on jubilantly. "Together we are making Snow Valley Secondary a place that celebrates kindness and care, creating a community for each and every one of us!"

A few people clapped and Owen closed his eyes, needing to block out at least one of his senses.

"Okay, without further ado, Ms. Atkins, please begin today's presentation."

Because his eyes were still closed it took a moment for Owen to register that something was off. Instead of the usual cheers and applause that greeted the photos of the Explorer groups, a deadly hush had settled across the huge room.

For a moment Owen did not want to see what was on the screen because this could be it, the axe. And when he finally looked, he just saw the presentation title page introducing the Explorer's Day slides and the school logo. But then Owen read the logo and he sat up straight, his heart slamming against his rib cage. Because instead of the usual "Snow Valley

Secondary: Where Students Create, Learn, and Grow into Responsible Citizens," it said something different. Very different. The slide that was lit up in front of the entire middle school said:

"Snow Valley Secondary: Where Students Bully, Lie, and Get Away with It."

What was going on? Owen glanced at Gemma but she seemed as thunderstruck as Owen.

Gasps and hushed murmurs spread across the room when the second slide popped up on the screen. It was a photo of Cody with a stamp across it that said, "Bullied so much he left Snow Valley Secondary for good."

Something was going on, but Owen didn't know what the blackmailer was trying to accomplish. And so far, it didn't have anything to do with secrets or the four of them.

"Stop the slideshow immediately," Principal Grace shouted at Ms. Atkins.

"I'm trying but—" Ms. Atkins floundered, just as the third slide appeared on the large overhead.

This one was in panels. The top panel was an email from Cody's father to Principal Grace with the story of the clothes stolen in gym class highlighted. The second panel was a response from Principal Grace, a whole week later, promising to "investigate the incident immediately."

The next slide came up with a picture of James and the caption, "The incident was not investigated until today, when the administration was forced to confront clear evidence of what happened. So who's the real bully here: James or Principal Grace?"

Owen gasped out loud.

"Why can't we stop the slides?" Principal Grace raged from the stage, his face bright red. He had pushed Ms. Atkins aside and was desperately stabbing at keys on the laptop that no longer appeared to be controlling the PowerPoint.

"I think it's been set to automatic," Ms. Atkins said. Ms. Montenegro was simply staring up at the screen, as the talking in the audience of students grew louder.

"What is happening?" Ally asked in a strangled whisper that Owen barely heard.

Owen felt the same way he had felt the day he'd gone sledding and somehow crashed chest-first into a lamppost. His mom had called it "getting the wind knocked out of you" but it felt a lot more like his lungs had been flattened.

A slide with a split panel appeared, two more instances of students bullying Cody. One was a social media post from a few days after the gym incident by a girl named Tara that said, "Last guy on Earth I'd date: Cody." There was a shriek from the middle of the auditorium that Owen guessed was probably Tara, but he couldn't tear himself away from the screen to check. Next to it was an email from Cody's mom to the principal stating that Ryan had been telling Cody he "ran like a little girl" and that others in the class now mocked Cody daily.

Owen felt slightly sick at this—he'd had no idea people had been so cruel to Cody. Why hadn't the principal done anything?

But the answer to that came on the very next slide. It was an email from Principal Grace to Ms. Montenegro saying, "Word of bullying cannot get out or the school will no longer be eligible for the Gold Star. Ignore the emails—parents exaggerate. I'll speak to the teacher."

Principal Grace was going ballistic up on the stage, running around trying to find a way to unplug the overhead screen. Ms. Atkins was following in his wake, trying to help, and Ms. Montenegro still stood frozen, staring up at the screen.

Around them people were reacting and scraps of conversation bounced around the large room.

". . . messed-up . . ."

". . . poor Cody . . ."

". . . they let him suffer just to win some stupid award?"

"Who put all this in the presentation?"

It was the last statement that galvanized Owen because of course it had been him. Him and Todd and Gemma and Ally. This was the file they'd planted on the principal's computer! "PP" stood for PowerPoint and they'd downloaded it to a folder called "Explorer's Day," which was clearly where the principal had stored the presentation. But instead Ms. Atkins had played this one.

"We have to get out of here," Owen hissed to Ally, who had turned to stone next to him.

Todd and Gemma were up so Owen grabbed Ally's arm and the four of them hustled out of the auditorium, leaving behind what was turning into total chaos as more slides appeared.

They hurried around the corner and then slipped into an empty classroom.

"You guys, this is a takedown of Principal Grace,"

Gemma said, her voice higher than normal. She was twisting a lock of hair around one finger so hard that the tip of her finger was turning white. "And I don't think Vivi's the one behind it."

Neither did Owen, not anymore. Vivi loved the principal and had called Cody a loser more than once. She'd never come to his defense like this.

"Whoever it is, they aren't done," Ally said, sounding slightly out of breath. Owen hoped she wasn't hyperventilating. "Their final move with the spotlight hasn't happened yet—and we have to stop it."

Owen nodded. Ally was right—whatever was coming next was bound to be the worst thing yet.

"So if it's not Vivi doing all this, who is it?" Ally asked. She had what Owen's stepdad would call a "deer in the headlights" expression, like she knew something awful was bearing down on her but it was just too much to comprehend.

As soon as Ally asked the question, Owen knew the answer. It was something he himself had said when they were making the recording. At the time it hadn't registered as a clue but now it was the missing piece to the puzzle.

"Ms. Montenegro," he said breathlessly.

Gemma gasped. "You're right! She was supposed to get the principal's job this year, that's what she said, but he's staying on and she's stuck in her old position until he chooses to leave!"

"So she figured out how to get rid of him," Todd said grimly, punching a fist into his palm. "All right then, let's go."

"Where?" Owen asked.

"To her office," Todd said firmly. "And we're not leaving until we find the evidence to prove that she's been the one behind this all along."

ALLY

As Ally ran down the hall after Todd, Gemma, and Owen, a cold sweat prickling her temples and her whole body shaky, there was one thing she could not stop thinking about: Cody. Seeing his picture made her remember something that had seemed so minor at the time that she'd forgotten about it. But learning about all the bullying he'd endured had her suddenly wondering if maybe it hadn't been so minor to Cody. He'd been in her English class last year, a kid who didn't say much but every now and then tried to make people in the class laugh. It generally didn't go very well and once it had gone quite badly. And the thing was, it had been Ally's fault. She hadn't meant to get the whole class yelling at him. But when he said the book they were reading, *Call of the Wild*, was stupid because animals didn't have feelings, Ally had quickly corrected him with a lot of facts to prove him wrong. As it happened, there were plenty of passionate pet owners in the class who were offended by Cody and energized by Ally's facts, and the whole thing had turned into a Cody-bashing fest. Ally had felt bad at the time but now—now she felt awful. Because Cody had been picked on by everyone in school and instead of helping him, she had—unknowingly, but still—made him the target of the whole class.

They reached the main office and this time Ally only hesitated the tiniest bit crossing into the no-students-allowed section. Because if they didn't find the blackmailer, what did it matter if she was caught in Ms. Montenegro's office? She'd already be on her way to prison for stealing Buttons and expelled for hacking the principal's computer. Todd led the way to Ms. Montenegro's office and once inside, he began issuing instructions.

"Owen, go through the desk drawers. Gemma, do a careful check of what's open on her computer now. Ally, you and I can go through these files." He gestured to the stack of files on Ms. Montenegro's desk.

Ally wondered if anyone would protest Todd taking over, but no one did. They were probably all as shell-shocked as she was about the presentation and the reveal that Principal Grace, head of the anti-bullying campaign, had tried to cover up bullying at their school. It was unbelievable and yet it had happened—the slideshow had proven that.

Owen knelt in front of the desk while Gemma stood next to him, gingerly moving the mouse on Ms. Montenegro's computer. Todd picked up the files and carefully handed the top half to Ally.

"We should remember what order they're in," he said, and she nodded. It was kind of hard to hold the folders because she was shaking and now even her palms were sweaty. Ally could not remember ever feeling this level of terror. Her family and her home and basically her entire life were on the line. But it was no time to give in to panic so Ally wiped her hands on her jeans and gripped the folders hard. It was time to focus.

Though as she opened the first folder, doubt started creeping in. Ally wasn't actually sure Ms. Montenegro was behind this. Why would she need a group of students to get those clothes and put them in James's locker for her? Couldn't she just expose the file of Cody emails herself? But the biggest question in Ally's mind was, even if Ms. Montenegro was evil enough to blackmail them, how had she found out all their secrets? Though in fairness, how would *anyone* have found them all out?

That was why Ally wasn't expressing her doubts—it could have been anyone yet it was nearly impossible to imagine someone capable of actually doing it. The person had to have incredible hacking skills that would include uncovering Principal Grace's password, have amazing planning abilities considering this had been started weeks ago, with the blackmailer fishing Cody's clothes out of the garbage—and in addition to all that, be able to sneak around school undetected all day.

"Ms. Montenegro is really into snacks," Owen said, holding up a plastic-wrapped set of powdered dough-nuts. "This drawer is full of them."

"Don't eat any of them," Gemma ordered.

Owen looked insulted. "I would never do that."

Ally sat on the chair in front of Ms. Montenegro's desk. Todd was leaning against the edge of the desk and had already gone through two files.

Ally looked down at her first one. It appeared to be full of bills but she paged through quickly, even checking the backs, in case anything was hidden there. She was about to open the next one when Gemma spoke up.

"Guys, come see this," she said from her seat in front of Ms. Montenegro's computer. Ally set the files down carefully, in order, then went back around the desk to look at the screen.

"Okay, so there's this," Gemma said, clicking on an open document that was a letter praising Principal Grace and recommending him for some kind of life-time achievement award in education.

"That could be a cover," Todd said, but he sounded unsure.

"Right but then there's this," Gemma said, clicking on Ms. Montenegro's email—not her school account but a private one. "Don't worry, her email was one of her open tabs so she won't know we looked at it."

They all leaned forward to read the message to a woman named Delia, who seemed to be either a good friend or relative of Ms. Montenegro's. In the message Ms. Montenegro complained about Principal Grace staying on, saying much of what she'd said on the phone, but then went on to say that Principal Grace had been her mentor and biggest supporter.

"She even calls him her role model in school and in life," Gemma said with a sigh.

"Gross," Todd muttered.

Owen sagged against the wall behind Ms. Montenegro's desk. "So I guess she's not out to get him after all. And we are out of suspects."

Ally wasn't shocked, but this revelation left her filled with despair. Now they were out of suspects and if they didn't find the blackmailer . . . Ally was now nearly coated in sweat and her hands were shaking so much she clenched them together behind her back.

"Who else could it be though?" Gemma asked, sounding more anxious than she had ever sounded, at least in the short time Ally had known her. "Who else feels so strongly about bullying? Or has a reason to bring the principal down?"

"Maybe it's Vivi after all?" Owen asked, pressing a hand to his forehead.

"Are we positive it's not Ms. Montenegro?" Todd

asked. He was rubbing at his temples like his head was hurting.

"But what would be her motive if he's her big mentor?" Gemma asked, closing up the email so Ms. Montenegro would never know it had been opened.

"Maybe this is all a cover and she has some kind of deep-seated grudge against him?" Owen suggested.

At his words Ally froze. What he had just said—it reminded her of something. Something that she'd heard on the recording when they'd listened to it earlier, something that if she could just remember, would be the clue to crack this case.

"Or maybe she has an evil twin," Gemma said. "Guys, come on, it's not a—"

The mention of a sibling did the trick. Ally pressed her sweaty hands in front of her chest and stood tall.

"You guys," she said. "I know who it is! I know who's been blackmailing us this whole time!"

GEMMA

"Let's hear it," Gemma said eagerly. She was starting to feel desperate because they *had* to find this black-mailer. There was no alternative.

"Dana!" Ally said gleefully. "The blackmailer is Dana!"

"Dana?" Gemma asked, looking more closely at Ally. Ally did not look great: She was oddly damp and she kept waving her hands around. Gemma hoped Ally actually had a theory and wasn't just losing it.

"I think she's right," Owen said excitedly.

"Well, I don't know what she's talking about," Todd said crossly.

Ally was practically vibrating with excitement and, instead of standing still, began pacing around the small office, her hands wild. "Okay, let me start at the beginning: At first we thought the blackmailer was someone out to get James. Then at the assembly, we found out it was bigger than that: Someone was out to take down Principal Grace."

"Right, we were there, you don't need to back up that much," Todd said, clearly on the brink.

"Okay, so what links together not only James and Principal Grace but also the four of us?" Ally said, looking around like she now expected them to see what she saw. "Think about the recording—it's all on there!"

"Cody," Owen said. He'd closed the desk drawer and was standing next to Todd.

"Cody!" Ally practically shouted like she hadn't heard Owen. "Cody is the link! Everyone impacted today did something to bully or at least upset Cody and they're—we're—the reason he had to leave to go to boarding school. So that means the blackmailer—Dana—is doing this to get revenge for all the bad things that happened to Cody."

Gemma scowled because Ally's theory didn't make sense. "I didn't do anything bad to him and you didn't either." Gemma also had no idea who Dana was yet, but one issue at a time.

"When I saw his picture in the slideshow, I remembered I accidentally embarrassed him in class last year," Ally said. She'd finally stopped waving her hands so much but her forehead was shiny with sweat. "And everything else is in the recording we made: Todd punched him, Owen dumped him as a friend, and you turned him down for movie night. James humiliated him and Principal Grace is the biggest bully of all because he knew Cody was suffering and didn't help him."

"Why didn't this revenge person just make slides of us, then?" Todd asked.

"Because there was no paper trail," Ally said, slapping her hand on the desk. This was something Gemma had heard on TV shows but had never heard someone actually say. "The people in the slideshow—what they did was documented, in emails and stuff. But the things we did—there's no record of them."

"Yeah, but a lot of people probably did stuff like we did that wasn't a super big deal but still bothered him and this person isn't blackmailing them," Todd pointed out.

Ally shrugged impatiently. "Maybe they didn't have secrets that could be used for blackmail or maybe Dana *is* going to blackmail other people too, I don't know. The point is, she chose us today."

"So who is this Dana getting revenge for Cody?" Todd asked.

Ally stopped pacing and was now bouncing on her toes. "Owen told us, in the recording—he said Cody's family is really protective of him," Ally explained. "Especially his sister, Dana!"

And now Gemma got it.

"She must have started planning this a while ago, when the principal didn't do anything to help her brother and he had to leave for boarding school," Owen said, almost as excited as Ally. "And remember, she works in the office so she has access to the computers here. Hacking to get information, maybe following us or asking around about us, or—I don't know, the point is she found the information she needed to pull this off and to get us to do her dirty work and get justice for her brother."

Gemma was the one clapping her hands now as she tried to keep from shrieking in delight because Ally was right: The blackmailer had to be Dana!

"You are a genius," Todd told Ally. He was grinning as he turned to Owen. "And I guess that recording wasn't a waste of time after all."

"I think it's safe to say it was pretty genius as well," Owen said, grinning back.

"So now we have to find her before she does whatever she has planned as her spotlight finale," Ally said.

Gemma nodded, hoping it was not too late.

"And make sure she never tells our secrets to anyone," Todd added. "But how do we find her?"

Ally and Owen weren't the only geniuses in the room because now Gemma was the one remembering something from the recording.

"Guys," she said, bouncing on her toes. "I know exactly where we can find Dana and catch her doing exactly what she told us she'd do: steal the spotlight!"

"What?" Owen asked, his brow crinkled.

"We thought she was using that phrase like a drama metaphor but she meant it literally," Gemma explained. "That spotlight was the most expensive thing the school bought with the parent donations and Dana is going to get her last bit of revenge by stealing it—and framing someone else for the theft."

"Like us?" Todd asked in a deadly voice.

Gemma felt a chill at this because if they were too late—

"Maybe," she said, starting for the door. "But whoever she's setting up, we have to stop her."

"But where is she?" Ally asked, her voice shrill.

"She's up in the lighting booth that the drama club uses," Gemma said as they hurried out of the principal's office.

"Wouldn't the teachers have already checked there

to stop the presentation?" Ally asked, bumping into Owen because she was looking at Gemma instead of where she was going.

"No, they'd have checked the tech booth but that's behind the stage—the lighting booth is upstairs and it's only used for plays and stuff," Gemma explained. Her membership in drama had come in handy, despite Owen's criticism.

"Let's go!" Owen called, and the four of them raced down the hall. Once at the auditorium they snuck in the back—which was not hard because everyone was milling around, talking, with Principal Grace still on stage shouting—and Gemma led them up the back stairs to the lighting booth.

Which was when they got what might have been the biggest shock of the day. Because the person in the lighting booth unscrewing the spotlight from its stand was not Dana.

The person in the booth—the person who had been blackmailing them this whole time—was Cody.

CHAPTER 9

MONDAY: 2:32 P.M.
OWEN

Cody was standing over the spotlight holding a screw-driver, but when he heard them he leapt into action, locking the door moments before Todd threw himself against it.

Owen could see how shocked Cody was—his eyes were wide and he kept blinking as if he couldn't believe the four of them were actually standing on the other side of the door's glass window.

"There's another door, hurry," Gemma said, her voice tense as she took off.

But by the time they had rounded the corner, Cody had locked that one too. He appeared to have recovered from his surprise and now he smirked at them.

"Open the door!" Todd shouted.

"No chance," Cody said, his voice slightly muffled by the door wedged shut between them.

"I can't believe *you* were the one blackmailing us," Owen said. Sure, Cody had been kind of intense and obsessed with things being fair back when they hung out. But this was extreme. Owen was honestly a little impressed Cody had been able to pull off such an elaborate scheme.

"What choice did I have?" Cody asked, his face tightening, his eyes hard. "You saw what happened to me at this so-called Gold Star school. I had to expose Principal Grace—he let bullies ruin my life here and now I'm getting homeschooled."

Ally glanced at Gemma. "I thought you were at boarding school."

Cody nodded. "Who do you think got that rumor started? I didn't want people thinking I just ran back home to cry because they drove me out. I needed them to think I was somewhere fun until I could expose the truth about what really happened to me."

Yeah, this really was an impressive feat Cody had pulled off. But that did not make it okay, at least not to Owen.

"You made us do your dirty work," Owen told Cody indignantly.

"Yeah, thanks for that," Cody said smoothly. Owen

wished he could reach through the door and give Cody a shove. A hard shove.

Clearly Todd felt the same because he slammed his hand against the door. "You're not getting away with this."

Cody held open his arms and gave a look of fake confusion. "I don't know what you mean—I already did."

"Not stealing the spotlight," Gemma said. "You haven't done that and you're not going to." She was standing between Owen and Ally, fists clenched.

"And you're definitely not framing us for taking it!" Todd added.

Owen nodded vigorously. Cody had gotten away with a lot today, but at least they were going to stop him from doing this.

Cody raised a brow. "You did what I needed you to do today," he said. "I have no reason to frame you for anything. We're done. Which means you can leave now—I won't do anything else to you."

"We're not going anywhere," Owen said firmly.

"That light might not matter to you, but it's the school's. Taking it would hurt lots of students who were excited about it," Gemma said. "So it's not happening, not on our watch."

"That's the point," Cody snarled. "This place hurt me—I have every right to exact some revenge. And I don't need you interfering with it."

"Tough," Todd said, grinning. "Because that's exactly what we're doing."

Gemma whipped out her phone. "I'm texting Mei to tell a teacher to get up here fast—that we've discovered a crime in progress."

"And the person responsible for the Explorer's Day slideshow," Todd added. "You're going down, Cody."

Owen could not help smiling at this. Stopping a crime felt good! Especially after you'd been forced to commit a few yourself.

"You have no evidence I'm behind anything that happened today," Cody said in a way that reminded Owen of a snake slithering silently across his backyard.

"We have all the texts you sent!" Todd said, holding up his phone.

Cody shrugged, smiling. "There's no proof I sent them," he said. "But an awful lot of proof you followed those directions."

This unfortunate truth settled like a rock in Owen's stomach. Even Todd remained quiet.

Cody rubbed his forehead for a moment. "Okay,

well, I guess we're done here. And don't worry, your secrets are safe with me."

With that he bolted for the far door.

Owen led the charge around the corner, nearly crashing into the water fountain, but by the time they arrived, Cody was gone.

GEMMA

"Mr. Patel," Gemma said, looking at the evidence Cody had left by the spotlight he'd intended to steal: Mr. Patel's cell phone in its extremely distinctive case with a map of the world wrapping across it and a small HISTORY ROCKS sticker on the bottom. "He was framing Mr. Patel."

After failing to catch up with Cody, the four had returned to the lighting booth to see the one Cody plan they had managed to foil.

"Why would he set up the nicest teacher in school?" Owen asked. His cheeks were pink from running. They had moved fast but Cody, without the spotlight, had moved even faster. And since there was an exit right down the stairs, he was long gone.

"They got into a thing last year," Gemma said,

remembering the story Mei had shared. "Mr. Patel thought Cody cheated and Cody went ballistic over it."

"I remember that," Todd said, nodding. "Everyone in class got mad at Cody too."

"Which is just the kind of thing he holds a grudge about," Owen said, lifting up the paper coffee cup from the Snow Valley Diner. The exact cup Mr. Patel brought to class every day and that Gemma suspected had his fingerprints on it, just in case the phone wasn't enough. Because Cody was nothing if not thorough.

"They're not," Ally said out of nowhere. At least that's how it felt to Gemma, who was still trying to sift through all that had happened in a very short amount of time.

"Who's not what?" she asked, pushing her hair back from her face.

"Our secrets aren't safe with Cody," Ally said.

"Yeah, you're right," Owen said. "Sooner or later he'll use them against us again."

"Or just expose us because he feels like it," Ally said. She was leaning against the wall, her face obscured by shadow because the light in the booth was off.

Gemma had a sudden thought. "Do you guys think . . . do you think he even knows what our secrets are? I mean, he never said, we just assumed what he knew."

"I don't know," Ally said slowly. "It's possible he was at the shelter and recognized Buttons. She's kind of a distinctive dog and he might have known her owners."

"But how would he have known about the checks?" Todd asked, his fists balled up.

"Maybe he hacked into the bank records to find out if there was any dirt on you," Gemma said. "But how could he know if you forged your grandfather's signature? For all he knows your grandfather lives with you and has very similar handwriting."

"It's hard to believe he could figure that out, but it wouldn't be impossible," Ally said. "Like if he was really investigating us there is a lot you can find out online."

Gemma wasn't buying that: Seeing her with Miles was one thing but knowing Todd had forged checks? Cody wasn't a mind reader.

"He probably could have figured out about James pretty easily," Owen admitted, and Gemma almost grinned. Except she was too furious. Was it really possible that they'd done all this when nothing was at stake after all?

But then Ally spoke again. "It's possible he knew our secrets and it's also possible he lied. Or somehow figured out we had things to hide, even if he didn't know all the details. But in the end it doesn't matter." She held up a hand as they all spoke at once. "Really. I mean, we already did what he wanted and we all believed he figured out we were each hiding something. And to me that just proves what I said before: Our secrets aren't safe. Maybe Cody knows them, maybe he doesn't, but obviously we all think it's possible someone could find out the truth someday. I mean, that's been giving me nightmares ever since I took Buttons."

Gemma thought about this and realized it was true. Their secrets were never going to be safe—honestly they never had been. And for the first time it occurred to Gemma that her problem wasn't her secret, it was the fact that she'd lied. She'd lied to her parents and to herself: She didn't want to be in drama club—she wanted to play basketball. And then there was the fact that Gemma had been lying to her friends for months. Which pretty much meant that the one thing she'd taken for granted about herself and taken pride in—being a good friend—kind of wasn't true. At least not since Miles.

As Gemma stood with Todd, Ally, and Owen in front of the lighting booth, something wild occurred to her: Cody had actually done her a favor today. Thanks to everything that had happened, Gemma knew it was time to be done with lying for someone who wasn't a good friend to *her*. And to start being a true friend to the people in her life who deserved it. And she knew exactly where she needed to start with that—though it was most definitely not going to be easy.

"So what do we do about it?" Todd asked angrily. His face was hard and his eyes were flashing. Which made what Gemma had to say that much harder.

"We don't have a choice," she said, trying to use the same calm voice Ally used. "We have to come clean."

"Not happening," Todd said firmly. No surprise there obviously. Which Gemma got—Todd had more at stake than any of them. But his secret was the most dangerous—he and his mom were vulnerable, and for him to keep avoiding that truth was just going to make it worse. Gemma had been worrying about this since he had revealed his secret. She knew Todd would not want to hear what she had to say about it but that was okay, she'd deal with getting yelled at for a friend.

"Ally's right," she told Todd. "Someone else could

find out your secret at any time. And Todd, you and your mom need more than just money."

The wrath in Todd's expression was so intense Gemma had to look away to continue. "You guys need real financial security and your mom—she needs help."

She cringed a little when she saw how Todd clenched his fists, shaking because he was so full of rage.

"Mr. Patel's wife is a lawyer. I bet we could go ask him for advice about the checks," Gemma said. "Since we saved him from getting fired or arrested for stealing the spotlight, he's going to be around for a while. And he can probably also help you find your mom a good psychiatrist who doesn't charge too much—I know some even see certain clients for no charge."

"Maybe if your mom got help and you didn't have to take care of everything, you wouldn't be so angry all the time," Owen added.

He stepped back when he said it but Gemma was still impressed, both by what he said and the fact that he'd said it even though Todd was now a seething volcano of fury.

"You guys don't know anything," he spat. "And don't ever say my mom is crazy."

"That's not what—" Gemma began, but Todd held up a hand as he stared at her hatefully.

"I'm done listening to you," he said. "All of you," he added, making sure to glare at Owen and even Ally, who hadn't spoken. "Don't say a word about my mom again, not ever."

"Okay, but—" Gemma tried again.

"And let me ask you this," he went on, his voice full of spite. "Are you going to tell everyone about Miles? And Owen, are you coming clean with James about how you ratted him out?"

"Yeah," Owen said, shrugging. "I'm tired of being worried about it all the time. He'll get mad but whatever. You guys were right—he really isn't worth my friendship. He's mean and what he said to Henry was racist and neither of those is okay."

"And I—" Gemma began but yet again Todd interrupted.

"Your secret is stupid anyway," he told her. Gemma knew he was mad but that still stung a bit. But if Todd thought she was just going to give up on him because he yelled a little and hurt her feelings, well, he had no idea who he was dealing with. Gemma wasn't going to be done with this conversation until she was happy with the outcome. Because thanks to what had happened with her uncle, Gemma knew she was right about Todd's mom. And she wouldn't be living up to her new pact if she didn't help him see that too.

Todd turned to Ally. "But your secret is real and you get what I'm saying, right? You're not just going to roll over like these guys, are you?"

Ally cleared her throat. She looked calm as she spoke.

"Actually," she said. "I am."

ALLY

It wasn't just that Cody might have known the truth—it was everything that had happened that day, starting with skipping out on class and ending with leaving an assembly without permission. Ally followed rules, it was who she was. But today someone had used her secret to pressure Ally to break rules, to do things she didn't want to do, things she knew weren't right. She'd done them anyway, out of fear. So when they'd confronted Cody, Ally had seen something big and important, something she hadn't seen before. As long as she had something to hide, she could be pressured into doing things she didn't want to do. She would have to choose between a secret revealed or doing what she was told she had to do. So hard as it would be, she was going to have to reveal her secret and do her very best to never have another secret like it again.

"I don't want anyone else to be able to blackmail me," she explained now to Todd, who was still fuming at Gemma's words.

Todd looked as if he wanted to take her head off over that but instead he turned a scathing gaze to Gemma, who had her phone out. "Texting your boyfriend?" he snapped.

"Actually I'm doing some research," Gemma replied coolly. "Ally, the penalty for adults who dognap in New York State is up to six months in prison or a fine of up to one thousand dollars."

It was a good thing Ally was near the wall because her legs were no longer able to hold her up. There was a reason she'd never done this search before.

"Wow, you're a big help," Todd said, his voice thick with sarcasm.

Owen stood behind him looking anxious.

"I'm not done," Gemma said. "The penalty for

misdemeanor animal abuse is a year in prison," she went on. "And for aggravated abuse it's two years plus a fine of up to five thousand dollars."

Gemma looked up from her phone expectantly, but Ally's brain was still stuck on six months in prison.

"Ally, the punishment for what they did to Buttons is way worse than the penalty for dognapping," Gemma explained happily. "And that's not even taking into account the fact that you took Buttons to *save* her."

Ally nodded but still wasn't putting it all together.

"There's no way they're going to want to press charges against you because the charges against them would be so much more serious," Gemma said, understanding that Ally needed it spelled out. "So if you go to them, maybe with a lawyer or mediator or whatever, and say you have Buttons and you won't press charges if they won't, it will be over."

"It will be over," Ally repeated, as it clicked into place. It had never occurred to Ally to think about the fact that the people who'd owned Buttons had broken the law too. And that the truth coming out could hurt them more than it hurt her.

"Gemma, you're amazing!" Ally said, so overcome with relief she rushed over to hug Gemma, who surprised her by hugging her right back.

"I'm just a good researcher," Gemma said, grinning, when Ally let go.

"You could be a lawyer," Owen told Gemma seriously.

Gemma nodded. "It's a possibility."

But the relief Ally had felt was now overcome with a gut-twisting realization.

"My grandparents are going to be so upset with me." Just imagining their faces, what they would say when she told them, made Ally want to hide in that janitor's closet for the rest of her life.

"Yeah, but they love you so they'll forgive you eventually," Owen said. "Believe me, I know, I mess up a lot. My mom and Big Rob get mad but they get over it."

Gemma snickered at this but then she looked at Ally. "We all get to make mistakes sometimes," she said.

Was that true? Ally had a sneaking sense that it might be. Her grandparents did love her and it wasn't just based on the fact that she mostly did the right thing. So it stood to reason that, yes, they'd be mad, like Owen said, but like Owen also said, they'd get over it.

"And the sanctuary will be safe," Ally said out loud.

"Yeah, definitely," Gemma said.

It was going to be okay. Ally could hardly believe it, but it was true. Yes, it would be hard to come clean to her grandparents but they would forgive her and she'd make it up to them. And together they'd go to Buttons's former owners and put this behind them for good.

Now Ally looked at Todd. She'd been so wrapped up in her secret she'd barely followed what he and Gemma had been saying. But seeing how angry Todd was made Ally realize that until they figured out a way for all of them to come clean, it wouldn't be completely okay.

"Todd," she said softly. "If we can figure out my problem, we can figure out yours. Can't you let us try to help?"

"Yeah, some of us are geniuses, remember?" Owen said.

"Others of us might become lawyers," Gemma added.

All three of them looked at Todd, waiting to see what he would say.

TODD

Todd opened his mouth to tell them to stuff it. But other words came out instead. "I've already done the research and it's up to ten years in prison for falsifying a signature on a Social Security check," he said, his voice brittle. "And the fine on that is real: two hundred fifty thousand dollars."

Owen gulped a little at these numbers and Ally bit her lip but Gemma just nodded like she already knew. Which she probably did, he realized, given how she liked to stick her nose in other people's business—she'd probably looked it up right after researching Ally's problem.

"That's for an adult though, and extenuating circumstances matter," she said, like she had a legal degree already.

The lava in Todd's stomach bubbled at her know-it-all attitude. "Not enough," he said through clenched teeth. "It's a crime and if it's found out, I'll have to pay and Mom—"

Something awful was happening. Instead of furiously telling them that Mom would be upset and hurt and might even lose custody of him, Todd felt his throat clogging up. And from out of nowhere he was blinking back tears. It was probably because the hall outside the lighting booth smelled like a mix of pine and sweaty socks.

Ally reached out to squeeze his arm while Owen moved closer and hovered, clearly wanting to be helpful but not sure how.

Todd blinked as hard as he could and when he'd managed to clear his eyes for a moment, he saw that Gemma was looking at him. Not judging or worried or freaking out. But like his reaction made sense.

"My uncle Paul came to live with us during Covid," she told him. Todd had no idea why she was going off on a tangent but he was grateful to have a moment to get himself back under control. "He's got depression and he talks about it a lot. At first he thought he was just sad and needed to get over it. He was married to my aunt Lydia and she would get frustrated with him because he'd never want to do stuff and hardly talked to her. She told him he was depressed but he thought depression was just being weak and that he could handle it."

This story was actually not helping Todd at all. Hearing it made his insides more Jell-O-y and his throat was still tight. But he didn't tell Gemma to stop, mostly because she wouldn't, knowing Gemma, but also because he wasn't positive he wanted her to.

"So finally Lydia left and Uncle Paul just kind of collapsed. He stopped working and cleaning up and wouldn't pick up the phone. My mom went to his apartment—he was in Philadelphia, and I remember she was gone for over a week. She got Paul to a psychiatrist and he told Paul that depression has nothing to do with strength of character—it's brain chemistry and DNA and all kinds of stuff you can't just get over or whatever."

"Oh, that's like Jade, my sister," Owen said. He was standing so close that Todd could smell the meat loaf from lunch on his breath. This should have annoyed Todd but for some reason it felt okay to have both Owen and Ally right there next to him. "She has anxiety so she takes medication and goes to therapy to rebalance her brain. It works pretty well because she's very chill. At least when she's not hogging the computer," Owen added.

"Yeah, that's exactly what Paul says," Gemma said. "He needed to learn some new ways to understand himself and also take medication so that the chemicals in his brain were more balanced."

"And that made him better?" Todd asked, skeptical.

"He would say no, that you don't cure depression, you learn to manage it," Gemma said. "He's working again and has a new girlfriend and a cat and he says he's more himself than he's been in years. And—"

Gemma leaned forward to emphasize her words. "He says the smartest decision he ever made was to get help. He says he wishes everyone knew that depression isn't something to be ashamed of. It's not like you did something wrong or you're weak and that's why you have it. It's not something you can control: You need help to manage it and when you get it, it changes your whole life and makes you you again."

"It sounds like he has a lot to say about it," Todd said. It also sounded like everyone in Gemma's family were know-it-alls just like her.

"We all have a lot to say in my family," Gemma said with a grin, confirming this suspicion.

"Everyone needs help sometimes," Ally pointed out. "I need it with the mess I made taking Buttons."

"I needed it to realize that it's time to quit drama club and go back to basketball," Gemma added.

Owen reached a hand out for a high five, which Gemma landed with a loud smack.

"I needed it when I got stuck on our garage roof and my parents had to call the fire department," Owen said. "And when I crashed our family computer and Mom said I had to pay for it but Jade got it working again." He grinned ruefully. "And I probably shouldn't have needed it to know James was a bad friend, since I saw him be racist and mean, but thanks because I guess I'm someone who needs extra help sometimes."

They were all laughing at that. But then once again, Todd found all three of them looking at him to see what he was going to say.

"I'll think about going to Mr. Patel," he said.

The bell rang and they all jumped. Todd had almost forgotten that they were in the hall above the assembly that had gone very wrong.

"Okay," Gemma said. "Let's go find him now. You can decide we're right on the way."

They weren't letting him get out of this. And they weren't leaving him to do it alone.

"You're really pushy," he told Gemma. But then he rested a hand on her shoulder for just a moment. "Thanks."

OWEN

Owen bounced his way down the stairs, tripping a little on the bottom step.

"You look like Goofy," Todd told him. Owen grinned but did not explain he could not help bouncing. That was what happened when the weight of a worry you'd been shouldering for months fell off—you bounced a little when you walked.

"What *is* Goofy?" Owen asked instead. "Pluto's the dog."

"My aunt told me he's a cow," Ally said. Owen noticed she was bouncing a bit as well. Maybe they all were. "And my aunt knows everything."

"A cow," Owen said thoughtfully. "I could see that."

They arrived down in the auditorium where the students had mostly cleared out. The stage was empty but still lit by the final slide that said, "Time to get ALL the bullies out of Snow Valley Secondary."

Owen paused and rubbed his hand along the back bench as he stared at it. "You know, I'm not going to say I'm okay with Cody blackmailing us, but he did have a pretty good reason to expose Principal Grace."

"Cody's a maniac," Todd said, which was not exactly a surprise.

"He is but what happened to him was pretty unfair," Ally said. "And he kept trying to get help from Principal Grace and was ignored—he had to do something."

"But he didn't have to mess up our lives," Gemma said. She glanced toward the last few students standing at the side of the auditorium and Owen noticed that one of them was Vivi. "And like, I get that he was mad at us for things we did but I had the right to say no to movie night. And Ally, you get to speak up in class."

Owen's insides were a bit squirmy at that. "I could have been nicer," he admitted.

"Well, he had that punch coming so I'm not sorry," Todd said. "But Principal Grace was definitely the real bully and I hope he gets fired."

Owen didn't see how the principal could keep his job after what Cody had revealed. And while the others had a point about Cody not needing to drag them into it, he could kind of get why Cody had.

"You know," Ally said slowly. "I'm angry at Cody—we all are. But he doesn't seem okay—I think maybe we should tell Mr. Patel to get someone to reach out to him too."

"The same Mr. Patel he tried to frame?" Owen asked, feeling protective of his teacher. But Ally had a point. "Yeah, Cody does seem like he could use some help too."

Gemma was nodding and Todd didn't protest.

Vivi and Sophia were walking by and Vivi looked teary. Owen suddenly remembered that today her hard work was going to pay off and even though he knew it no longer mattered, he could not stop himself from calling out to her. "Hey, Vivi, what's up?"

"Shut up, Owen," she snapped. "I bet you're glad I lost out on being Gold Star Assistant."

"On being *what*?" Owen asked. He heard Todd snicker.

"At the end of the assembly Principal Grace was going to announce the student chosen to help win our school its second Gold Star Award and it was going to be *me*," Vivi said, like it was some big honor. Owen had never heard of it, or if he had, he'd forgotten about it because it sounded stupid.

"I don't think our school's in the running for that Gold Star Award anymore," Gemma told Vivi with a small smirk.

"You think?!" Vivi hissed, then stalked out, friends in her wake.

"Poor Vivi," Todd said with mock sympathy, and they all laughed.

Owen's phone vibrated in his pocket and he pulled it out, enjoying how freeing it felt not to worry about being blackmailed. But when he saw who it was from, he frowned.

"James?" Ally asked, because apparently she was a mind reader. Though Jade did say that she could tell everything Owen was thinking just by looking at his face. After the day they'd just spent together, Ally probably knew him nearly as well as Jade.

"Yeah," he said, stuffing his phone back in his pocket. "I'll call him after we're done talking to Mr. Patel and tell him about the test stuff."

"Caden and those basketball guys are going to ice you out tomorrow," Todd said.

"Yeah," Owen agreed. "Good thing I have other friends to hang out with."

"You have other friends?" Ally asked. "I've never seen you with anyone else at lunch."

"Duh, you guys are my friends," Owen said.

Sometimes Ally could be thick. "And I'll be at lunch tomorrow with you guys, at our table, so I'm good."

"We have a table?" Todd asked. His voice was casual but Owen could see that his eyes were shining.

"Yeah, the corner table by the window," Gemma said. At least someone had picked up on the obvious.

"Right," Ally said, and then she smiled a very big smile.

"So now let's go to Mr. Patel's room before he leaves," Gemma said, starting toward the door.

"Hold on," Owen said. "There's just one last thing we need to do." He took out his phone again and with the three of them watching, deleted the recording they had made.

"Okay," he said to his friends. "Let's go."

ACKNOWLEDGMENTS

I am forever thankful to have the fiercely fabulous Sara Crowe as my agent and ally. Pippin Properties has a roster of stars—Cameron, Rakeem, Ashley, Holly, and Elena—who have supported this book every step of the way, and I am one lucky duck to have them in my corner.

Emily Seife is magical in her ability to improve everything I write, and I am so happy to get to do another book with her. The Scholastic team made this book and they made it beautiful. Maeve Norton designed a cover I adore; Stephanie Cohen, copy editor, and Priscilla Eakeley, Lara Kennedy, and Nicole Ortiz, proofreaders, gave the book its much-needed final polish; and Janell Harris, production editor, kept it all on track—no easy feat in a pandemic. I am indebted to all of them!

Big shout-out to the friends who support me in my writing and in my life—I couldn't manage either without you: Marianna Baer, Kira Bazile, Debbi Michiko Florence, Donna Freitas, Lisa Graff, Deborah Heiligman, Carolyn MacCullough, Alexa Murphy,

Josh Phillips, Marie Rutkowski, Jill Santopolo, Eliot Schrefer, Rebecca Stead, and Martin Wilson.

My mom is my reading rock star, sharing her love of books throughout her life with family, a generation of students, and the entire town of Tivoli, New York, when she joined the library board. My dad's beautiful use of language and passion for a good story forever inspire me. Hugs and much gratitude to my sister and teammate for life, Sam; my brother, Nghia; and my most magnificent nephews, Khai, Avi, Shiloh, and Dash. Kisses, chocolate, and so much love to my husband, Greg, and sweet sixteens Erlan and Ainyr—you guys are as good as it gets and I will always keep your secrets.

ABOUT THE AUTHOR

Daphne Benedis-Grab is the author of the middle grade novels *The Angel Tree, Clementine for Christmas,* and *Army Brats,* as well as the young adult book *The Girl in the Wall.* She is the part-time school librarian at PS32 in Brooklyn, where she gets to hang out with kids and books all day (she is a very lucky person!). She lives in New York City with her husband, two teens, and a cat who has been known to sit on her computer if he feels she has been typing too long. Visit her at daphnebg.com.